Blood Tide

by Larry Grubbe

Prologue

The ocean, a living breathing contradiction...without it, life doesn't exist; disrespect it, and the enormous liquid can kill. Care for it, and the ocean gives a bounty, gives life – a truism Jacob Brittles' father always re-inforced before they went fishing or diving off the Oregon coast. As they left the protection of the harbor, he would finish his lecture with *Respect all conditions whether she is calm or in a rage.* Captain Jake Brittles was always teaching.

Chapter 1

The mission started under the cover of darkness, seventy-five miles off the coast of San Diego. The Fast Response Cutter *Reliance* had been at a disadvantage. Shortly after leaving port, the radar system malfunctioned. The cutter had been patrolling for two weeks.

The sun had long disappeared below the horizon. They spotted the devils after midnight, heading toward shore. The captain ordered the 26-foot *Over the Horizon IV (OTH)* into the water. Petty Officer Jacob Owens Brittles and three of his shipmates in the OTH had seven miles of angry Pacific to maneuver. The *Reliance* would follow far behind.

The bow of the OTH punched through the three-foot swells. The white caps sprayed stinging frigid water over the windshield. Jacob buried the throttle, pushing the OTH to its limits. The constant pounding numbed the body and mind. The bow rose and descended, gallons of water cascaded over the bow, the frigid salt water sloshed, bow to stern. Larsson quickly turned on the bilge pump,

Jacob's crew was familiar with this routine; they had taken down a half-dozen narco boats this year alone. Outwardly, Jacob showed confidence shouting out orders as they sped away from the Reliance, leaving it far behind. Deep inside, his stomach churned. The danger was always there, even though Jacob and his shipmates had successfully taken down multiple drug runners in the past.

"Check your gear men," Jacob said. "Ensign Wills, load up the M240. We might need to send a message!"

"Semper Paratus," Wills said.

"What do you see Larsson?"

Ensign Larsson wiped the wet lenses and salt water from his eyes and lowered his thermal night vision goggles and he saw the heat signatures of the narcos boat and crew. Focusing, he seen the waves crashing over the bow of the thirty-footer. Three men sitting on a bench seat behind the driver, held on for dear life.

Larsson laughed. "The boat is getting tossed around like a toy… Wait, hold on, they are slowing down."

The OTH was close, Jacob pulled the throttle back to neutral and coasted to within a hundred feet of the narcos.

"They stopped, there is movement on the deck," Larsson said.

Jacob took a deep breath, wiped the salt water from his face… "Get ready we might have to jump on board to stop them," Jacob said.

Jacob fought to keep his mind on the dangerous mission at hand. Kate always crossed his mind and what would happen to her if he bought it. What if he was disabled? His mind raced until the mission objective came back into focus. He idled the OTH forward. Larsson handed him the night vision goggles.

"Be ready to board, they might start dumping the load, I'll get closer."

Three men stood at the stern of the thirty-foot speed boat staring into the empty Pacific.

"What are these clowns up to? Jacob mumbled reaching for the bull horn. This is the United States Coast Guard, Detener, Detener Ahora!" Jacob yelled.

Before Jacob uttered another syllable, the Pacific exploded in light and fire. A trail of red tracers pounded the windshield of the OTH. Seconds later, the windshield shattered, glass shards invaded the OTH. Jacob and crew dropped to the deck. Bullets and red tracer rounds ripped two-inch holes through the two-layered aluminum hull.

"What in the hell are these fools doing, do they have a death wish?" Jacob screamed. He lay on the deck, warm blood trickled down his face into his mouth, the cold salt water surging into the OTH burned his face. His heart wanting out of his chest. "Is anyone hit?"

Looking back for his crew, Larsson and Rodgers were face down and not moving; Jacob turned away, his soul pained. He crawled over glass toward them. He grabbed Rodgers' arm and shook it.

"Rodgers, Rodgers! can you hear me?" Nothing. Warm blood drained from Rodgers' arm and chest; red water pooled. Jacob put his head over Larsson's chest. Not a beat. The narcos' relentless gun fire teared through the hull above and below the water line. The OTH started to list toward starboard, as a steady stream of water flooded the deck. Jacob did not dare raise his head as bullets pounded in and around the boat.

A faint groan from the bow pulled his attention forward. "Wills, you hit?"

"Yeah, bad," Wills mumbled.

Jacob took a deep breath, inhaling air thick with smoke. He spit up blood and water, his chest tightened. "Hang on, Wills. I'll get us out of here."

Heartbeat surging through his ears, Jacob lay on the deck. Black smoke insisting on invading his entire body, would not yield. His throat narrowed, seeing the instrument panel and radio no longer existed. A jolt of adrenaline rushed through his shaking body. He reached up and punched the throttle forward. The OTH engines sputtered, spit out a cloud of grey smoke and idled away. He didn't care where, he just wanted away from this death trap.

Jacob peered over what was left of the engines. The speed boat and five submersibles were in pursuit and closing fast. His pulse quickened.

Jacob's chin went up after he had put some distance between him and the narcos slow submersibles. The speed boat was closing fast. He stopped the 26-foot OTH and crawled over Wills into the bow, as bullets punched holes through the transom. He turned OTH around and faced his pursuers, Jacob wanted the big thumper, the mounted M240. He leaned onto the machine gun, hair raised on the back of his neck. He grabbed hold of the trigger in one hand and ammo in the other. Two heavy thumps forced him off his feet. Jacob lay on the deck gasping for air. No clean air to be had, choking he raised up. His body armor was damaged but saved him. Dazed and gasping for air, he staggered back to the M240.

Light from a full moon pierced the black Pacific as red tracer rounds buzzed past him, he triggered the machine gun and let it do its business. Jacob screamed, "You fools feeling frosty, see if you can handle this heat."

The drug runner's dove for cover...the ones still able. Jacob fired with precision, and the armor-piercing rounds showed no mercy. He reloaded and kept firing, sweat rolled down his forehead. His forearms tensed; his fingers numb.

"You fools, no mercy today. Time to meet your maker!" he screamed. He fired every last round they had, after the last bullet left the 240, an eerie silence filled the smoke-filled Pacific. The narcos had been silenced. Jacob closed his eyes and collapsed onto the shredded seat cushion. A painful ringing filled his ears.

A warm beam of light touched his face, the sun found its natural position, peeking over the horizon, revealing the carnage. Jacob scanned for life; his eyes burned. No movement from the Narcos. The smell of gun powered and smoke began to clear. He seen the side of his ship-mates faces; his friends Larsson, Wills and Rodgers lay face down in the water. Jacob held on to the rail, as the OTH rocked side to side. A blood tide covered Jacob's grief until the next roll of the OTH exposed their faces. He rolled them onto their backs and in desperation checked for a pulse. Nothing, shaking his head in disbelief, his jaw tightened, he leaned over his buddies. "Rest in peace." His eyes flooded.

Jacob's head throbbed, he sat dazed, his arms heavy, he strained to hold them up. He shook loose his agony as the once dark Pacific was fully illuminated. He caught sight of all the damage inflicted on the drug runners. The five subs and speed boat ripped into death and the OTH full of holes but still afloat. All were disabled. The metal and fiberglass hulls were ripped apart, lifeless bodies hung over the hatches of the subs, and the speed boat was engulfed in flames. He took a deep breath and removed his vest.

Jacob stood up staring at his enemies, from behind, a familiar sound rang out, a horn blast. The Fast Response Cutter *Reliance* appeared through the smoke like a calvary blitz. Jacob stumbled back a step, took a breath of clean air. The *Reliance* pulled close. Captain Stenson, Jacob's commander since his enlistment, and several armed crewmen stood on the bow. Jacob's legs wobbling, he made a sign of the cross on his chest, gave a halfhearted salute, and flopped back onto the shredded seat cushions, next to the machine gun and glared at the dead criminals, as they loaded the OTH back onto the *Reliance*.

* * * *

Captain Stenson stood behind a polished wooden desk. Pictures of ships, and people behind it. A large brass anchor with waves protruding from the sides was bolted to the wall under the portside window stood out, brass bells, and books rested on the shelves as light from the round port side window highlighted them and brightened the room. Petty Officer Brittles came to attention. "Have a seat Petty Officer Brittles," Captain Stenson said.

"Yes Sir."

"Officer Brittles, you, ok? Looks like a massacre out

there. Start at the beginning."

"Sir, in all the years the *Reliance* has taken down dozens of these narcos. I never thought they. . . He shook his head. Sir, Larsson noticed the speed boat had stopped. We figured they were giving up or had engine trouble. We coasted to within one hundred feet and stopped to assess the situation and all hell broke loose."

"The men in the speed boat opened up on you?" Captain Stenson said.

"The speed boat and the subs. We found ourselves surrounded. They all opened up on us at once Sir, it was a set up."

Captain Stenson sat down, balled his hand into a fist. "Your men, what happened?"

"Sir, they all went down in the initial engagement. I wanted to nuke 'um, sir, but my training kicked in,"

"It looks like it was a hell of a firefight, Officer Brittles. I want a full report, when we get back to port,"

"Yes Sir. This has never happened before; they always give up once we have them spotted."

"They have become emboldened by the rumors that the United States Government is going to default; sad to say, those rumors are no longer rumors. The U.S. Government announced the default three days ago."

Jacob's hand covered his mouth. "Never imagined, the rumors were true, sir."

"There's more – all branches of the military are being cut."

Jacob took a deep breath. "Us Sir?"

"The Reliance will be sold or mothballed along with

the entire crew; this is our last mission."

Jacob's chin fell. "Sir, mothballed? Just like that?"

"Yes, just like that! I understand this was going to be your career, but things change and we have to adapt – Semper Paratus."

"Yes Sir."

"It's a lot to take on considering your personal loss, the death of your mother a year ago and the recent disappearance of your father. Any word on your father?"

Jacob's throat tightened. His voice cracked. "They found his boat anchored in the abalone grounds south of Bandon, Oregon. The diver flag was out; his float tube nearby was half full of abalone. He was nowhere to be found. We dove there since I was a kid, never had a problem, Sir." Jacob stood at attention, forcing his painful chest straight, his eyes filled.

"I was holding out hope for your father. Sorry to hear the devastating details, son."

Jacob's shoulders drooped. "Thank you, Sir."

"Any idea what you might do next, Officer Brittles?"

"I have no clue. The family fishing business has always been an option."

"Good luck with whatever you decide, I will give you an outstanding referral if you need it. You have been exemplary for the Guard. Petty Officer Brittles."

Jacob saluted. "Semper Paratus, Captain."

Jacob departed. He took a deep breath and a heavy sigh as his head dropped. *I can't believe this, I just can't believe this is happening!* Uncertainty pained his soul.

Chapter 2

Jacob Brittles arrived at the Port of Bandon, Oregon, before the life giving, orange globe appeared. The salmon season had just ended leaving the docks eerily quiet. He was at home as he set foot on the deck of his father's boat, a 45-foot Bertram. It was clean and in excellent condition. His dad always kept it in immaculate condition, and Steve, his friend and fellow fisherman docked next to him, had kept it in running condition since his dad's disappearance. The galley, sleeping area, and small head shower combo below deck were more cramped than he remembered, but everything else was how he remembered it. Jacob opened the storage compartments on deck; the musty smell of rubber and fish smacked him in the face. The fishing equipment, diving gear and wet suits were neatly stored and in excellent condition.

His senses heightened, the fresh smell of the salt water, and the swoosh sound of air escaping the vinyl seats as he plopped onto the captain's chair. The wooden steering wheel was still smooth as silk. He had a rush of energy. He was ready to go.

The grinding of the starter, fired up the engine after three attempts, but once started it purred. Sitting in the captain's chair, Jacob reflected back, about his past connection to this boat and the Oregon coast. It consumed his childhood, fishing and diving with his father. Those days as a kid were not easy, Jacob would rather have been hanging out with his friends, but looking back. they were great times with his father.

Staring out the starboard window, something was missing, a pendant with a picture of his mother. Jacob's dad always hung the pendent there; it was the last picture of her sitting in the captain's chair, before she passed. He sat for a moment staring out the window, placing his hand against the window where the pendent hung and said a prayer.

The morning was cool with clear skies and a light breeze from the north. As Jacob pulled in the last docking line his head jerked back. Xian Chu and Han Lai, two of his closest friends and classmates from his college days at the University of Oregon were standing on the docks starring at him. He hadn't seen either of them in years.

Jacob shook his head. "What are you two doing here?"

Han folded her hair away from her face. "Kate called us a week ago, we sensed it would be a good time for a visit, how are you?"

"How did you find me?"

"We went by your parents' house; Kate said you would be here," Han said.

"You guys haven't changed much. Except Xian. You look a little long in the tooth," Jacob said, with a subdued laugh.

"Very funny, I see you haven't changed," Xian said.

"Man, it's good to see the both of you. Xian, why haven't you married this beautiful lady yet?"

Xian scratched the back of his neck. "Let's not go there."

"Long trip from Asia, huh?" Jacob said.

"Yeah, Vietnam recently," Han said. "How long you been back home, Jacob?"

Jacob had a rush of adrenaline. "Couple of weeks, long enough to reacquaint myself with the Bertram and equipment."

"We heard about you getting pushed out of the Coast Guard," Xian said.

"Yeah, my ship and the entire crew mothballed along with cuts in all branches of the military, rumor has it, up to fifty percent, but who knows for sure, government has defaulted they say."

"Tragic," Xian said.

"Great timing, you guys caught me at the right time." Jacob said.

"Kate told us about your father too," Han said.

"Yeah, I feel like the head of a nail – I keep getting hit. They found his boat anchored in the abalone grounds. His float tube was half full of abalone, but he was nowhere to be found."

"Still no word on what happened?" Xian said.

"No, I am just about to head out. You guys up for it?"

"Like old times, Jacob Owen Brittles!" Han said. "You still haven't married Kate, what's up with that?" A smile brightened Han's face.

"Where we going?" Xian interrupted.

Jacob cleared his throat. "Abalone grounds near the Shell Islands. We won't be out long, storm coming late tonight."

"Yeah, let's go," Xian said.

They cleared the docks followed by a few gulls. Blu, his Alaskan malamute, stood at the stern staring down the gulls, as they floated on the air currents behind the boat. Water lapped against the bow, as the Bertram cut through the calm water with ease, spraying a salty mist into the air. Sunlight sparked off the small ripples like stars in the night sky. The engine hummed behind Xian and Han.

"How long have you had the dog?" Xian shouted.

"Blu is Kate's, he's turned into my first mate."

"Like old times," Han said. Sitting on the bench seat behind Jacob.

"Yea, good times," Jacob said.

Before they knew it, they arrived near the Shell Islands south of Bandon. They were a half mile from the islands on the abalone grounds.

"How about we try some spear fishing?" Xian said. His hand stretched out, catching water spraying off the bow.

Jacob's head jerked back, his lips tightened, surprised to hear those words from Xian.

Xian had to be guilted into a dive in the past. Not today. The sea was calm and smooth like glass. Jacob's hair lifted on the back of his neck, he stopped the Bertram, this being the general area his father went missing diving for abalone. He made sure his friends didn't sense any hesitation, but his stomach churned.

"Get your wetsuits on and check the air tanks; I will drop anchor over by the point." Jacob idled forward, toward the outcropping of rocks. "Hey Han, don't forget the spear guns. I'm not going out there unprotected."

"Do you need an oversized hood to cover all that wild strawberry blonde hair, Jacob Owen Brittles?" Han said.

"Ha-ha very funny." *I guess I should comb it once in a while.*

Xian and Han were already in the water by the time Jacob got his suit on. He dropped anchor hundred yards off shore near an outcropping of rocks that jutted out from the point. Jacob wanted a quick dive to the underwater cave. I don't want to linger too long down there. Jacob thought.

He filled up Blu's water and food bowls, put out the diver's flag, checked his air gauge, and jumped in. They dove down twenty feet and started toward the outcropping of rocks. Han took the lead. She was an accomplished diver. She spent her summers diving and snorkeling on her uncle's boat back in Vietnam.

The Oregon coast is not the best for diving, or it wasn't until Jacob's father found the underwater cave while searching for abalone. It had to be some of the best diving and spear fishing anywhere in the world. The geography of the cave above and below the water line was amazing. The water inside the cave was crystal clear and warmed up, deeper into the cave. They guessed it was heated by a thermal source yet to be found. There was enough light from the small openings above for good visibility. The abundant sea life in the cave was always a surprise and varied.

Jacob scanned rapidly in all directions, as they entered the main cavity of the cave. His chest tightened thinking about his missing father. His mind raced... Did his father have a heart attack, did he get swept away by an over powering current, maybe a rock fell on him. Jacob didn't have the answers, it haunted him.

They were a few minutes into the dive as Han led them to a sand bar above the water line where they beached and rested.

"Do you want to explore deeper into the cave?" Jacob said.

"Yes, we have never been past this point, this cave is amazing; the water is crystal clear, let's keep going," Han said.

"A little farther? I guess won't hurt," Xian said.

Jacob led them deeper into the cave, his spear gun in the lead. Turn after turn they snaked through a tunnel ten feet wide and twelve foot high. The end of the tunnel opened up into an-acre oblong size lake, in a sixty-feet high cavern. Jacob's first sighting was a giant octopus crawling on the rocky bottom. Farther in, he noticed a few red rock crabs and some Pacific rock crab, sea urchin everywhere. Starfish clung to the rocks above and below the water line. The occasional rockfish and schools of surfperch circled the lake. Jacob had no idea what some of the creatures were. I'm sure straight-A student Xian, would give me the answer. Jacob thought.

They explored the entire perimeter of the lake, above and below the water line, and found a second sand bar at the rear of the cave where they landed.

"Hey look over there, a small opening, looks like the cave keeps going," Han said. "If we keep going, we might find the source of the warm water."

"Let's check it out," Jacob said.

"Not very wide opening, do we have enough air left?" Xian said.

"More than enough," Han said.

They glided on the surface and entered the passage-way. The beam from Jacob's head lamp lit the narrow cavity.

Xian stopped a few yards in to remove his mask. "I think we've gone far enough."

"What is that smell?" Jacob said.

"Rotting kelp, maybe fish," Xian said.

A few yards farther in, they saw where the stench came from, as a half-eaten sea lion carcass floated against the cave wall.

"OK, maybe a good time to get the hell out of here!" Xian's voice cracked.

"No time to waste," Han said, grabbing onto Jacob.

Jacob's mouth went dry. "Yeah, time to go, a shark shredded that sea lion."

Their heads turning on a swivel, they backed up to the wall of the cave, Waving the Spear guns side to side. Jacob submerged to see what was below, he seen no sharks. They did not hesitate and doubled-timed it out of the cave; spear guns out front.

Jacob took a deep breath and pointed toward the opening of the cave. *No sharks, thank GOD.* He shook his fist in victory; he wanted to take a victory lap as they hit open water. Jacob led Xian and Han toward the boat and safety, but he stopped, his body went limp. His victory lap hit a cement wall. They were in front of them and getting closer. Jacob's body tensed hard like a stone. He turned to Xian and Han; both breathing so fast, their excessive exhaust bubbles obscured their faces. They swam straight into a swarm of jellyfish; some of them must have been six feet long. Tentacles floated in every direction all the way to the surface. The strong current pushed thousands of jellyfish toward them.

Jacob pointed three times, the direction they would swim to get around the jellies and back to the boat. They swam south against the current three hundred feet and still were not able to clear the cloud of jellies. Jacob bit down on his mouth piece. *Never heard of this kind of swarm off the coast before; the giant jellyfish should be near China. Something is horribly wrong with this picture.*

They turned north, swam with the current for a few minutes and still, were unable to clear the cloud. Jacob's chest tightened. His legs burned, they stopped and rested, staring into the mass. His energy sapped; horrifying images attacked his mind... *What a nightmare.* The needle on his air gauge ticked closer toward zero. The tentacles of the jellyfish invited pain and death.

He was sure Han and Xian were tired and scared; the dive was long and tough, fighting the strong current. Something else had to be done. The jellies were thick and drifting closer. Jacob's mind was blocked, unable to move forward. He accepted the fact, there was no way around the bloom of jellies.

Jacob needed to get Han and Xian to shore. He was responsible for their safety. He was the captain. He didn't want to be responsible for them getting hurt. The boat would have to wait. He motioned to Xian and Han to surface. As they broke the surface, Han squeezed Jacob's arm. Xian stuttered something as he turned his head toward shore. Han took a deep breath, shaking in disbelief.

"We swam into a death trap," Jacob said. "Let's get to shore; it's too dangerous. I will deal with the boat later. Han, take the spear gun and lead the way."

Han led with Xian following. Jacob lagged behind and waited until they were out of sight and heading to shore. He turned toward the cruiser. No man or dog left behind, kept repeating in his head. Jacob was unable to shake the feeling of responsibility; he had to go back for Blu and the boat. It would be many hours before a rescue, if at all. The outcome would be catastrophic, especially with a big storm coming in tonight. The anchor would never hold through the storm.

Jacob dove down. The sandy bottom was clear of jellies. He swam in the direction of the cruiser pushing aside mounds of sand and seaweed while feet above him hung possible death. Jacob's enemy- the strong current fought against him. It would take every bit of strength he had left. The jellies were so thick, the light from above dimmed. He dreaded the idea of ascending topside through the translucent horde. His muscles tightened.

Every kick against the current burned. His legs drained of strength. The visibility on the bottom was no more than two feet. He scanned in all directions of his watery prison. He observed the sea floor littered with waste and old fish nets swirling in the current, another potential disaster. Seeing jellies in every direction, his breathing increased, heart beat invaded in his ears.

His wet suit protected most of his body except for two vulnerable spots – his face and hands. Jacob remained cautious with every dangerous stroke forward. His stomach churned with every painful stroke; he wanted to go back. Deep inside he knew going back was not an option. Blu and his family boat needed rescue. *How much worse can it get? Semper Paratus.*

Jacob had been scraping the bottom of the ocean for ten minutes, still no sign. He swam north in a half circle hoping to locate the anchor line. Thirty feet into the circle, he spotted a large gray shadow dogging him to the right. A violent thud resonated from his chest. Jacob wanted to hide. There was nowhere to go. His face heated, mask fogged.

The shadow moved toward him through the kelp and jellies, mirroring his every move. He stopped; it stopped. It was something big. Limited visibility tortured him, his head ready to explode. The giant continued to dog him. He pulled out his puny titanium knife and readied himself, for battle. The three-inch blade was sharp as a razor, only an eye shot would stop a giant, otherwise useless against this monster. The gray mass closed in on him. In an instant through the seaweed, the gray mass darted inches in front of Jacob. His heart skipped a beat. The force it created pushed his mask firm against his face and pushed him head over heels backward. A few feet above, the large sun fish ripped through the top of the giant jelly, like it knew what it was doing. Flesh floated in every direction as it feed on its prize.

Jacob laid on the bottom of the Pacific staring upward, kelp passing over his mask, thinking, *Thank God*, as his heart beat slowed. He reached for his oxygen gauge. The heavy breathing lowered the needle close to zero.

Jacob kept moving forward. As the stringy acid kelp swayed in the current, he detected by chance or divine intervention the anchor line swayed in front of him. His tank close to empty, at most a couple of minutes left if the gauge was correct. He had to act fast.

Jacob removed the tank and strapped it to the anchor line above his head. He ascended toward the surface; his head down holding onto the air tank. The long carbon fins powered him upward, his legs on fire, as he kicked with what little energy he had left. Praying the tank above his head would protect him from any stings. He scanned upward, a translucent army surrounded him, the surface was invisible. *Up there, my salvation.*

The jellies thickened, as he ascended. He doubted every decision he ever made. The slime engulfed his mask and wetsuit. The weight of the jellies inhibited his rise. Escape seemed impossible; they were relentless.

Forty feet from the sea floor, the air pressure needle dropped to zero. He took a deep breath. His legs fought him with every kick. His entire body burned. Every direction a curtain of slime, no openings. His lungs burned, as he inhaled the last breath. He was tortured, as he watched the exhaust bubbles float carefree upward toward the surface. He let go of the heavy tank and regulator. His head down, he pushed down with his arms and kicked with everything he had, he powered toward the surface like a missile, a missile out of fuel.

Just feet from the surface, Jacob came to a dead stop. He scanned this new world; only red string tentacles surrounded him. Paralyzed, his mind searched for answers, his heartbeat raced, temples pounded, his air gone. *Is this how it's going to end.* Time was slipping away; it would not stop to help Jacob. Jacob gave in and went limp. Like his prayer was answered, the giant jelly flipped over on its side, and Jacob floated out from its world, as the lifeless creature disappeared.

Jacob escaped the translucent prison, hitting the surface and gasped for air with jellies draped on him. He shook them off like a madman, as he climbed up the ladder on the stern of the cruiser. Slime dripped from his forehead. He gasped for air, his lungs hungry for oxygen. Jacob lay sprawled out on the deck for minutes, before he was able to breathe normally.

Stinging pain on his hand brought him to his feet. A welt developed; it started to itch then came a throbbing pain radiating up his arm. He went down to the galley and downed the antihistamine from the first-aid kit, found vinegar, and rushed topside to rinse with salt water.

Jacob didn't even notice Blu staring at him. Blu's head tilted with an odd look on his face. He gave Blu a pat on the back to assure him things were ok.

Jacob pushed past the pain and turned his attention to Xian and Han. He pulled the anchor line and headed closer to shore stopping just outside the breakers. He waved Xian and Han over to the point. "I'll pick you up there," Jacob shouted.

"Yeah, no problem," Xian hollered back. "There better not be any jellyfish out there, Han."

Han shook her head. "Should be ok; swim on top of the water, short swim from there."

Xian and Han trudged over the jagged rocks to the point, they waited for a swell to pass and waded into the water and swam forty feet where Jacob threw them a line and pulled them safely to the ladder at the stern.

" You guys, ok?"

"We good," Xian said.

"Xian, I need you to drive so I can check out these stings closer," Jacob said.

Below deck, Han-soaked Jacob's hand in vinegar. She used tweezers in the first-aid kit to remove the stingers. She found baking soda, made a paste, applied it to the affected area, and then shaved the area with a butter knife hoping to get any remaining unseen stingers. She finished by wrapping it with a bandage. Jacob sat, head down, staring at the bandage.

"Where did you learn all of this first-aid?" Jacob said.

Han stood in front of him. "Marine Biology class. As I recall, you were in that class with me, Jacob Owen Brittles. You did get your degree in Marine Biology, right?"

"Hmm, must have been absent that day."

Han smiled. "Don't think so Jacob." She put her hands on his shoulders and gave him a kiss on the cheek. "Do not scare me like that again, Jacob," Han whispered.

"I'm ok, I'm fine."

"We still taking you to hospital."

"Won't be necessary, I'm ok.

"We are still taking you to the hospital, no objections," Han said.

"I'm curious if the seal herd is ok; they should be on the beach south of the Shell Islands. We need to check on them," Jacob said.

"Yeah, I will check with Xian." Han peeked her head out from the galley. "Xian, Jacob wants to check out the seal herd on the island tomorrow, are you up for it?"

"Yes, our boss at AECEN and the local officials at INECE would be interested in what's going on here to," Xian said.

"Xian and I are all in Jacob," Han said.

Han, we have come a long way since college. Jacob said.

"Who would have thought a kid from a small village in Vietnam would be working at AECEN fighting against lawless criminals," Han said.

"I never imagined Xian would ever take the same career path as you did, Jacob said.

"It is a satisfying career," Han said.

Chapter 3

Old town Bandon was alive. The boats at the Marina bobbed up and down, the docks creaked and cracked from the passing storm. Jacob, Xian and Han boarded Jacob's boat after sun up. A slight breeze out of the west kept the ocean unsettled with small white caps waves. The ride out to the Shell Islands was slow. The smell of coffee infiltrated the wheelhouse as Xian and Han sipped their coffee. The enclosed wheelhouse protected them from the wind and the stinging salt water. While Jacob sipped on his coffee, he noticed Xian staring him down, shaking his head.

"I didn't want to mention this yesterday but, you are extremely lucky, Jacob! Do you have a death wish, you were down there a long time, we had doubts that you survived man," Xian said.

"Blu and the boat would not have survived out there with the incoming storm, and the anchor would not have held. The boat would have wrecked on the rocks and Blu might have drowned. I'm the captain and responsible for getting all of us home safe."

"Your life is more important than any boat?" Han said.

"Blu is part of the family, and the boat is worth more than just the 70,000, and it connects me to my family."

"Still not worth your life," Han said.

"I agree with Han, you crazy man!" Xian said.

"It had to be done; in my mind, I had no choice."

"This craziness seems like another one of your JOB moments," Han said.

"It sure looks that way. It was a scary swim back to the boat and it crossed my mind down there, on more than one occasion, I wasn't going to make it."

"Your God pulls you through or maybe you were just lucky," Xian said.

"I have no idea why these kinds of things follow me."

"I think you bring them on yourself; it's the reason you joined the Coast Guard, for the excitement it brings" Xian said, shaking his head.

"So how is life after the Coast Guard?" Han said.

"Been a major adjustment. I think Kate wants to kill me."

"Yeah, who wouldn't," Han said.

"Takes time to adjust," Jacob said.

The sea had calmed. Jacob slowed the Bertram just north of the Shell Islands. They did not see one seal on the beach. "This time of year, this beach is usually filled with seals. The swarm must have caused them to relocate." Jacob said.

"Possible. Seeing the giant jellyfish was strange; they're not native to this area, they are often seen off coast of China," Xian said.

"Yeah, something crazy going on," Han said.

"I can't believe the size of those jellyfish," Jacob said. "Some of them must have been six feet long.

Han dropped her head, a scrunched face, set her tone. - "Pollution and overfishing can cause these blooms, I realized what the pollution and overfishing back home can do to the ecosystem, I've seen it first hand while out fishing with my uncle, the over fishing is pure greed! The pollution is criminal" Han said.

"I can understand the native jellyfish being here, but why the giant jellyfish?" Jacob, said.

"Maybe the giant jellyfish... Cyanea Capillata, came with a strong current from the storm that blew through weeks ago," Xian said.

Jacob gave a nod. "You seem to have remembered more than I have from our oceanography class about jellies Xian!" A grin covered his face.

"What can I say Jacob, straight-A student!"

"It is also possible they are following a food source; the south China Sea is so over fished, I'm worried there won't be anything to fish for in ten years, the ecosystem is already in dire straits." Han said.

"I remember dad telling me that the water temperature appears to be changing and the currents were stronger; maybe that has something to do with the giant jellies being here." Jacob said.

"If that is the case, it could have an impact, don't forget Eutrophication," Xian said.

"What? I guess an explanation is coming," Jacob said.

"It comes from dumping sewage, and other pollution into the ocean. Basically, nutrient type pollution, this causes algae blooms and in turn jellies will increase," Xian said. "Xian, I think I need a nap after that explanation," Jacob said.

"I will call AECEN and see if they have any data on this," Han said.

"Jacob, Kate called us about what happened with the Coast Guard, we thought it a good time to try and convince you to join our sister group, INECE," Xian said.

"INECE. Not familiar with them," Jacob said.

"International Network for Environmental Compliance and Enforcement," Xian said. There are offices on the West Coast; Portland has one. If you are interested, you should apply.

"I'll look into it," Jacob said.

"A perfect fit, unless you are going into the fishing business," Xian said.

"I'll let you know. What are you and Han working on now for AECEN?"

"We've been trying to lock down the illegal shark fin trade," Han said.

"Important fight in your part of the world, Jacob said. "I've lived and fished here most of my life; dove for abalone here; this was our laboratory back in college! I have never seen anything like the jellyfish swarm."

"Crazy stuff," Han said.

"Where to now, Jacob?" Xian said.

"A beach, that way," Jacob pointed south.

* * * *

Jacob circled east toward the north shore of the island where they saw that hundreds of birds had invaded the Shell Islands sanctuary. Not a seal in sight and no signs of jellies in the water. What they did see, though, shook them to their core – thousands of dead jellyfish layered deep onto the beach.

Jacob drove the entire length of the beach. "What in

the world is going on here? One day there is thousands upon thousands of jellies floating offshore, now they're dead."

Han sighed. "Most might have already been dead, what a disaster."

"Let's head west and see if we can find clues for this craziness," Jacob said. Jacob's lips tightened as he turned the cruiser west. "Take the helm Xian, I'm going to get my wetsuit."

Xian piloted the cruiser due west for a couple of miles, where the surface water changed to a smelly thick soup. The engine bogged down as the prop struggled to turn. Jacob quickly turned the engine off. "What's going on with the engine?" Xian said.

A cold chill covered Jacob. "Looks like a thick soup of something might have clogged the prop. I'm going to net some samples."

Jacob dipped the fishing net behind the prop and pulled it back in dripping with goo.

"What is that?" Han said.

"It looks like jelly; the consistency is like. . . can I say this, a jellyfish," Jacob said.

"Is it dead jellyfish?" Xian asked.

Jacob took a whiff. "I haven't a clue. What's with the frown, Han?"

"I'll bet its part of the plastic trash that's been floating in the Pacific for years. I received information that it's starting to break down! Turning mush like,"

"How is it possible for the soup to make it to the West Coast, it's been stagnating in the middle of the Pacific for decades? I think this must be related to the swarm?" Xian said, scratching his head.

"We need to take samples and send them to INECE in Portland." Han said.

"I want to dive down and check the propeller and see what is going on under the surface," Jacob said.

The ocean was calm, as Jacob entered the water just outside the thick soup. The prop was wrapped in a dilapidated fish net and a thick goo substance. He spent five minutes cutting the net clear of the prop.

"Start the engine, Xian, and take it outside of the muck; I'm going to dive deep enough to get below the floating waste."

Jacob's jaw tightened down on his regulator. What he saw made him question if anyone was paying attention. He dove down further to see if any life existed below the muck, and sure enough – the giant jelly was there. He had to get a closer look. His wet suit covered him from tip to toe, this time no worries about getting stung, he got close, real close, this kind of opportunity does not come along every day. He circled the giant and inched closer, so close to the giant he wanted to reached out and touched it.

There was to many of the giant jellies to count, besides the giants there was fish and other jellies of all sizes, many trapped in the thick muck. The fish would be dead soon if they did not stop eating the miniaturized sized pieces of plastic and escape the soup. Jacob had seen enough and ascended to the surface.

Jacob removed his mask, took a deep breath. "Wow what an amazing creature, the giant jelly. Things don't look good down there. But the giant jelly is amazing. Xian, inflate the raft, while I get us close to shore," Jacob said.

* * * *

Jacob and Han rolled over three-foot waves, as they approached the beach in the inflatable life raft. Towering dunes enclosed the entire length of the beach. A solid wall of lifeless animals layered the beach, with no clear landing. A fierce wave forced them into a wall of dead animals and sand. The front of the rubber raft where Han sat disappeared under a wave. At the rear, a three-foot breaker undermined the raft and flipped it over. Jacob rolled a few feet on to the pile of dead and franticly struggled to his feet. Han dragged herself out from under the raft covered in sand and water. She spit out a mouth full of water and sand never letting go of the rope attached to the front of the raft.

Han glared down Jacob. . . "What the hell?"

"You never stop amazing me, your buried in water and sand and you still held onto the rafts rope," Jacob smiled. "You having fun yet?"

"You funny man."

Dead fish, birds, giant jellyfish and thousands of smaller species of jellies layered the beach with plastic of all shapes and sizes mixed, fishing lines and nets were the biggest culprit. The putrid smell covered Jacob like thick smoke and lingered as they got the raft turned and under control.

The dead animals were a foot high and twenty feet in from the shoreline across the entire length of the beach. Pushing aside the dead animals with a paddle, he bagged a couple of jellies, birds and some fish. Han struggled to pull the raft up the beach away from the waves. Jacob skated back to the raft, slipping and sliding the entire way. Han stood, rope in hand, her hair with gobs of sand and goo cascading down her face. She stared Jacob down, shaking her finger and swearing what he assumed were obscenities in Vietnamese. A deep guttural laugh exploded from Jacob.

"Why do you always get us into these situation's Jacob Owen Brittles?" she said.

"Just luck I guess," Jacob said spitting sand and salt water from his mouth. "Let's just get back to the boat; Xian must be getting anxious."

Xian stood on the stern, a smile on his face as they approached the boat. "I've been storing samples, didn't see you. It looks like you been in a war. What happened over there?"

"Yeah, we got more. Let's head south and see if we can locate the seal herd." Jacob said

* * * *

The seal herd was a mile south on a remote beach. Jacob glassed the entire beach with his high-powered binoculars. He spotted hundreds of seals grouped together; some were entangled in fish nets and fishing lines.

"We have a serious problem," Jacob said.

"Let me see," Han said.

"We need to help them out, they won't survive long."

"You're right."

"Let's get home; we'll overnight our samples to INECE and drive back to the beach in my truck tomorrow and see if we can help them."

"What can we do?" Xian said.

"If they are entangled in a net, or covered in goo, we can trap them with a sturdy circular net with a zipper on the side. You access the seal by pulling the zipper down exposing the area of net to be cut off. The seal's head will be kept in the net so as not to get bit.

"If we help just one seal, it will be worth it," Jacob said.

"Ok, if you say so," Xian said.

They docked the boat at the harbor, tied off the last docking line, as the sun disappeared over the horizon.

* * * *

Jacob and Kate arrived, five thirty sharp at Joe's Coffee Shop in Bandon. The aroma of coffee and pastries floated throughout the small room. They sat in a table near the front window. The shop was empty; the Barista delivered their usual. "Got some news," Jacob said.

Kate took a sip of her latte. "It, better be good."

"You tell me. Xian offered me a job."

"A job, what kind of job?"

"For a private company called INECE, working in environmental enforcement."

"Sounds too good to be true. Where? not in Asia, right!" Kate said.

"No, right here in Oregon,"

Kate took a sip of her latte. "Wow if it works out it would be a blessing."

"There they are now," Jacob said.

Xian and Han waved after seeing Jacob and Kate in the window. They greeted Kate with a hug, good to see you

Kate," Han said.

"Jacob tells us you are working for a Senator," Xian said.

"Yes, working on Senator Norin's campaign."

"That's great," Han said.

"He is big on environmental issues," Kate said.

Jacob shrugged, as his mouth tightened. "Xian, how long before they have results on the samples that we sent to INECE in Portland?"

Xian took a drink of Joe's house blend – black.

"Depends on how busy they are, no more than three days I suspect. They asked us to stick around until the samples are evaluated."

"What about our assignment in Vietnam?" Han said.

"Don't worry, it will still be there in a couple of days," Xian said.

Jacob's voice deepened. "What about the volunteers for the seals and beach cleanup today? We can't clean up all the plastic waste and dead animals and help the seals ourselves."

"They will show. I guarantee it," Xian said.

"How about you Han, you're awful quiet over there. You're going with us, right?" Jacob said.

"I'll go if you guarantee me no more JOB moments," Han said.

"This might be our last adventure together," Jacob said.

Han laughed. "Definitely, our last crazy adventure."

Chapter 4

Russia

The light of the freezing overcast day briskly faded, as the rioters marched to the Ministry of Agriculture building in Kazan. There were hundreds of desperate people looking for someone to blame for the lack of food and long lines for bread, meat available was only for the rich and well connected. The crowd in front of the Agriculture Building chanted, "Get out or die! This government must go!"

Fifteen military personnel guarding the building closed their ranks, blocking the front door to the building as the people approached. The soldiers did not hide the fact they were heavily armed. AK-74's, was a powerful deterrent.

The military's presence did not seem to dissuade the people. It only made them more determined. Thousands converged into the courtyard throughout the day; they were an intimidating force.

As darkness set in, the mob pushed closer toward the Ministry. Snowballs and rocks bombarded the guards standing under the archway in front of the metal tree, their freezing breaths floating together in the air as they shouted in unison.

People were angry, hungry and relentless. The expanding mass drew closer, like a balloon ready to pop, they closed to within fifty feet of the armed guards. The door to the Ministry building opened and a voice called out, "Do not let them in at all costs, Captain Brusilov!"

Captain Vladimir Brusilov was a decorated war hero, known by most military personal and familiar to the President of Russia, who pinned a medal on him for his bravery.

"No way they get past us sir," Captain Vladimir Brusilov said.

"Who's that, Captain?" Lieutenant Dmitri Dyakov asked.

"That is the Minister, Ivan Alexandrov, Lieutenant," Captain Brusilov said. "Crooked politician."

"What we going to do, Captain?" the Lieutenant said.

"This might get out of hand; hold your ground and follow my lead."

The people surged forward. Captain Brusilov removed his ushanka, wiped the sweat from his brow. He had no choice. He had his orders. Captain Brusilov jerked his head back, took a deep breath. He fired his AK-74 in the air, and his men did the same, hoping to dissuade the mob. The noise alone stalled the mob for a moment then, desperately they charged. A chill flushed through Brusilov. He hesitated, staring at the rioters in shock, his face tightened, as they rushed toward the archway. He shook loose his disbelief and fired into the crowd; his loyal men following orders did the same. The deafening sound of gunfire echoed throughout the city.

The bullets ripped through flesh. The wounded fell, some crawled away; many lay motionless and bled out on the frozen ground. The screams from the rioters were muted from relentless gunfire. The advance was stopped. The people still alive panicked and scattered in all directions.

Brusilov moved forward and perched himself on the top step of the Ministry like a conquering king who had just won a battle. He watched as the rioters panicked; many people were pushed to the ground in the chaos. People lay there, some screaming unable to get up as the masses swarmed over them. Many who fell were trampled on by thousands of people fleeing the gunfire. The firepower from their automatic weapons proved deadly in more ways than the obvious. After the gunfire stopped, hundreds of people were lying dead and wounded in the courtyard. Captain Brusilov stood out front and ordered his men to reload and be ready

The rioters dispersed behind two brick buildings. One building to the west and one to the east, provided cover. Behind the buildings, two men in a covered delivery truck, with the name Baranov Meat written on the side were handing out Molotov cocktails to whoever would take them. "Two for every man willing!" a man on the truck shouted.

The rioters circled to the east and west of the agriculture building with gas filled bottles. The rioters hid behind bushes, cars and small buildings. They were in range for a quick dash toward the archway. A single shot echoed throughout the courtyard. Seconds later the sky lit up like a New Year's Eve celebration. Hundreds of cocktails floated toward Brusilov and his men.

They fired a few short bursts toward the crowd, as the flaming cocktails tumbled toward them. The captain and his men ducked for cover as fire fell. Captain Brusilov and Dmitri made it into the building; other soldiers' dove for cover behind garbage cans and the two wooden benches.

The cocktails landed simultaneously all over the front of the building. The wrought iron tree in the archway was in flames. Gunshots rang out, as the small arms bullets riddled the front of the ministry. Small gas fires burned throughout the ministry building. Two of Vladimir's men hiding behind the old wooden benches were rolling on the ground on fire. The second the sky cleared Vladimir pushed through the front door and ordered his men to follow.

Vladimir's adrenalin flowed; hair rose on the back of his neck. He ripped off his ushanka, throwing it to the ground. His veins protruded from his forearms from clenching his gun tight. He raised his weapon. He advanced gun to chin, his men eased forward with him. "Fire! Fire! Fire!" Vladimir shouted. They charged down the snow-covered stairs into the courtyard firing wildly in all directions with their high-powered weapons. The smell of gun powder strong in the air, shell casings carpeted the ground.

Within minutes, hundreds more lay dead and wounded. The screams were deafening. The courtyard once covered in fresh snow, turned blood red, the likes of which Brusilov had never seen before. Even his battles in the Middle East were not this bloody.

Brusilov and his men pushed the crowd back from the

agriculture building. They were no match the military's fire power with just Molotov cocktails and small arms fire. Brusilov, being a seasoned soldier and seeing this kind of revolt in other countries, knew this was not over. He ordered his men to continue the pursuit.

They chased after the crowd, opened fire on them as they retreated, leaving many more people dead in the streets. Only lack of ammunition stopped Brusilov and his men from killing hundreds more.

"Hold your fire!" Captain Brusilov yelled. "Stand down men!" They stopped the chase in the middle of the court-yard. His chest thrust out; he stood tall scanning the courtyard, as smoke and fog stagnated low around him. With a hoarse voice, he shouted... "Get back to the trucks and reload, they might be back."

Brusilov a confident solider, walked back to the agriculture building proud of his men. They followed orders and stopped the lawless bunch. He strolled past the fountain in the center of the courtyard, something caught his eye; it stopped him in his tracks, his knees weakened, his face heated as he fell to his knees. A sharp pain punched his gut. Emptiness overtook his soul. He stared motionless like a statue, as large snowflakes layered his uniform.

Vladimir's eyes fixed on a woman and young baby lying next to a broken wooden bench in the center of the courtyard next to the fountain. Their faces were disfig-ured and bloody, the baby's legs and arms bent in all directions. The mother's neck was bent backward. Frozen cemented blood covered the blonde hair of the woman and child.

Both had been trampled to death by the fleeing crowd. They lay there in a pool of blood and red slush, the baby's head protruding from under the mother shoulder, legs twisted around her head like a toy doll.

"Captain, let's go! you're exposed over there," Dmitri said.

Bullets from small arms riddled all around Captain Brusilov and Dmitri.

Vladimir turned away and did not respond. He stared at the woman and baby shaking his head. Vladimir untangled them and held their hands as bullets started hitting the wooden bench next to him. He turned away and stared into oblivion, Vladimir Brusilov soul left him. He laid down next to them and stared at the mother and baby until darkness and snow covered their faces.

Dmitri kneeled next to Vladimir. "What's going on sir, why are you doing this?"

Vladimir said nothing.

Dmitri and two men pulled him away from the mother and child and forced him back to their trucks, under the cover of darkness. Sirens blasted throughout the courtyard as ambulance after ambulance raced in.

Vladimir sat in his truck mumbling to himself all the way back to the barracks. Major Popov, his superior, stood outside the truck door staring at Captain Brusilov through the window. He propped open the door. Popov reached out to Vladimir and ripped off his captain's bars and ordered him taken away – no explanation, straight to the stockade and solitary confinement. Vladimir had no response. He stood in his cell like a dead man, no expression of any kind.

The major shut the cell door and shook his head. Brusilov you are one lucky man, your past in the war has saved you from many years in prison. The President has ordered us to be lenient with you. . . "You have two choices, Brusilov. One, you can resign your commission in disgrace without pay and pension, spend time in the stockade or take a single man post on the shore of Okhotsk pumping fuel for the Coast Guard as a Private. Maybe in thirty years you can retire with a pension. If it was up to me, you would be in prison for life! The choice is yours. Take it or leave it."

Vladimir sat on a cold metal bed; his eyes stared at the cement floor. He wanted to hide, sweat rolled down his forehead. "I'm a decorated war hero, the president himself pinned the metal on me and this is what I get! I don't care about anything anymore. Do what you will with me."

"You will pump gas and like it," Popov said.

Chapter 5

Vladimir stepped off the train in Okhotsk, to a blistering cold day. He had to maneuver a few blocks of deep snow before he reached his barracks. The bitter cold numbed his face, and his thin coat was no match for the wind and snow. His cold hands struggled to turn the door knob into the barracks. No family was with him, as he had none left. The empty barracks reeked of mildew. He dropped his gear onto a cot and settled into the frozen one-room barrack overlooking the docks. He turned on a small electric space heater near the back wall. The heat struggled to overpower the cold frosted room. The one window on the south side, covered with ice and snow, blocked the outside world from entry. He laid out on the bunk wanting death. He crawled under the one blanket, closed his eyes and passed out.

The next morning, he woke to his new reality. Vladimir's orders were to fuel any ship that showed up, nothing more. After his first week, he hadn't seen one ship to refuel or any military personal, so he spent his time wandering Okhotsk's shores and docks. The wooden docks were weathered; large cracks and splits were prevalent up and down the main dock. Sheets of ice were beginning to from on the shore line. The sun did not live here.

The docks were busy, fishing boats coming and going. Next to the docks, buildings with roll up doors lined the street. Every dreary cement building, stacked one after another.

The sights Vladimir seen shocked him. People were hunting rats for food, beggars surrounded fisherman coming in from their days fishing, hoping for a fish head or tail. Escaping this hell tortured him.

Vladimir soon realized the military didn't care if he lived or died here. He had no food supplies, and zero ships came by to refuel. He searched for ways to make an extra buck to buy fresh fish. Scrap metal and old copper pipes discarded by the military made him a few rubles from the locals.

His daily routine took him to the docks looking for food and anything to make life bearable. Most days he came back emptied handed. A shortcut, back to the barracks would take him through an alleyway behind the docks. Where he would find things, businesses discarded. Extra scrap wood from broken pallets used for a fire was top of his list, and on occasion he found loose paper or, if he was lucky, a half-eaten piece of fruit. He had to get there early or things would be picked clean; others were always there searching.

Day after day, nothing changed for Vladimir. Every morning at five, he walked the same street on his way to the fuel depot. He spent all day and into the evening waiting, hoping for any boat to come in to refuel, but none came.

The light of the day was long gone before Vladimir woke up from his daily snooze at the depot. This day was different; a letter was shoved under the door. Private

Brusilov opened the door, hoping to see someone, a bag filled with rice and beans was there.

Private Brusilov was written on the front of the letter, no return address. Vladimir gripped it tight. He tore off the side of the envelope. The top of the letter read- "Sorry to inform you." Vladimir's heart raced. The lettered continued- "Your wife and child have been cremated and the ashes have been discarded." His faced flushed as he slammed the letter against the wall. His stomach churned and sweat began to soaked his shirt. He stared at the letter for minutes and then set it on fire and let it loose into the wind. *Never again, will anybody, take everything from me, ever.*

Snow blew sideways past the cracked window in the depot. He struggled to shut the door behind him, as he left for the barracks. He turned his face away from the blistering wind; his thin coat no match for the frozen hell. He headed into the alley protected from the wind by buildings on both sides. He noticed three men cooking some strange smelling meat over a barrel, while a fourth... slept on a pallet. Vladimir walked head down toward them hoping they might make a trade for something to eat and get a little heat from there fire. He put his hands over the fire and rubbed them together.

"Hey there men, do you want to make a trade for..." Vladimir staggered away from the fire, his head spinning from a blow to his forehead. He regained his footing, throwing punches of his own. Another fist from his left side to his temple put him to his knees, and a kick to the back of the head put him under.

Vladimir woke shivering, his hands tied behind his back. "What the hell you doing, I'm in the military, there will be hell to pay?" he yelled.

A short stocky man stood up and kicked Vladimir in the stomach and sat back down on a wobbly wooden three-legged chair.

"Shut up, or we might just eat you," a deep wrinkled face said. They all laughed.

Vladimir's blood rush to his face. His stomach churned.

He spit toward Deep Wrinkle. He was rewarded with another kick to the head from the short stocky man.

"Now how are you going to taste with blood and snot all over you?" Loud laughter echoed down the alley; liquor continued to flow between them. "We want your fuel," Deep wrinkle said.

"It's not possible," Vladimir mumbled.

"If freezing to death is what you want then so be it," Stocky man said.

Vladimir's body quivered, and stars danced inside his head, heat flushed through his body. He sat on the wet ground shivering, and said no more, his captors passed around a bottle of vodka, each chugging enough to kill a small child. The last drops drained down Deep Wrinkle's beard, he tossed the bottle at Vladimir, breaking it on his knee. Deep Wrinkle staggered into a shelter made from wooden pallets, two others followed, another lay next to the fire, on a pallet. While his captors slept, dead to the world, drunk., Vladimir crawled close to the fire burning in a fifty-five-gallon drum,

Shivering and half-frozen, the rusted drum gave life back to his hands and feet. Once the fire in the barrels subsided and cooled, he placed his hands through a jagged rusted hole in the drum, and sawed his hands free from the stiff frozen ropes. Then the soldier in him came out and he made his move.

These drunken idiots picked the wrong man to mess with.

Vladimir pried off a large piece of the rusted drum and cut the rope around his ankles. He sloshed through the snow over to Deep Wrinkle, who had passed out and was snoring. Vladimir sat on his stomach and woke him with one hand over his mouth and the rusted metal tip at his throat. Vladimir made sure the man knew who it was. He stuck the rusted metal through his throat and ripped up to his ear. Blood rushed out of his neck. Wrinkled Face gargled blood out of his mouth, as he mumbled something incoherent. A violent shaking followed, then silence.

White beard eyes opened, Vladimir hovered over him, his foot pushing down on his stomach. The rusted metal dripped blood onto his face. White beard staggered to his feet and grabbed hold of his throat. Vladimir held him up, pulled his face close, White beard was no longer white beard, he was red beard now. Trembling violently, he fell to the ground and laid there silent and bled out.

The third man, short stocky had it the worse. Without hesitation Vladimir slit a hole in his stomach and ripped up to his neck, his guts spread on to the ground as the man screamed and twitched wildly. Vladimir stepped over his body, twisted his foot on the man's innards on his way to the last victim. The fourth man woke and ran; Vladimir punched him in the back of the head. He went down, falling on his back. Vladimir put his foot to his neck and jammed the rusted metal in his heart and left it protruding from his chest.

Unnerved, Vladimir snagged the small piece of meat left on a stick over the smoldering flames. Covered in blood, he turned and saluted his victim's, as they lay in the red slush and calmly walked out of the pitch-black alley.

* * * *

Vladimir stopped at the front door to the barracks and before entering his shack, he broke off an icicle and applied it to the rope burns. The room was cold as death. He lay there thinking how ruthless life is. He almost lost his life in the alley. On top of seeing the poor beggars eating rats and fish heads, he promised himself he would never be put in that position ever again. He wanted out of this nightmare. Whatever it took, anything to escape!

Two days after the incident in the alley, local law questioned Vladimir but suspected nothing. Vladimir was relieved; he knew they would never suspect a decorated military man.

Weeks after the incident in the alley, Vladimir still had no boats to refuel and no contact with anyone from the military. He had much time to think. Vladimir obsessed with changing his circumstances and making money. Vladimir gave his life to the military and what did he have to show for it? A forty-year-old private working near nowhere. Everyday Vladimir sat in the five-foot-by-five-foot frozen fuel shed waiting for any military boat to stop for fuel. No one ever came, but staring at him – pulling at him – was a grave yard of old abandoned ships and boats, some were docked, others half sunk, some run aground just across the narrow inlet from the fuel shed. One of them was a rusted whaling ship, that stood out.

Vladimir waited for the sun to set, wishing time would speed up. He eyeballed the whaling ship and many other old abandoned ships, some floating others half sunk, some beached. In the twilight, Vladimir started across the inlet in a leaky wooden rowboat. He pulled into a dock fifty feet from the whaler. A wooden ladder led up to the dock platform. Vladimir scanned the dock. Not a soul was in sight.

Vladimir strolled the rotten dock to the wheelhouse of the massive whaler. He passed by the long ramp at the stern of the whaler that led down to the water. The helm covered in weathered wood paneling, a wooden console and a rotted wheel stood out. A minor crack in the windshield and all the electronics had been scavenged, but the controls and gauges were still intact. Vladimir was surprised by how good things held up over the years. He made his way to the engine room passing by endless piping. He was shocked to see two engines mostly intact. The first thing Vladimir noticed was the hull of the ship, large swaths of rust littered the port and starboard sides and a few holes were scattered throughout.

Vladimir stretched his hands above his head. "Yes!" His shout echoed throughout the ship. The possibilities teased his mind.

He inspected of the rest of the whaler and was even more hopeful, the bilge was dry.

Vladimir rowed back to the fuel shed, his plan would not be easy.

Inside the fuel shed the heater had died, and the windows were fogged over. Vladimir sat staring at the walls and planned. He knew for his plan to work he had to get experience. Vladimir watched fishing boats come and go daily; one of them in particular stood out. He had one valuable asset to persuade – fuel. His choice an eighty-foot trawler, which unloaded a nice size catch on a semi regular basis.

The trawler – *Albatross II* – docked three hundred feet from the fuel shed. Vladimir chased down the man barking out orders, as he disembarked the trawler from his catch.

"Are you in charge?" Vladimir said.

"Yes, Captain Nabokov, want do you want?"

"I'm Brusilov. Private Brusilov. I have a proposition you might be interested in."

"I doubt it, but what you got?"

"I work at the fueling station for the military; I would like to learn the fishing trade."

"A lot of people would these days."

"I would be willing to provide you with all the free fuel you need, if you train me to fish and operate your trawler," Vladimir said.

Captain Nabokov's eyebrows rose, as he rubbed his chin pulling on his beard. "You got a deal. If we get caught, I will say you sold me the fuel."

"No problem. When do we start?"

"Be here at 4:30 tomorrow."

* * * *

Vladimir spent three weeks on the *Albatross II* learning. The deal with Captain Nabokov had paid off. Vladimir learned much in the short time on board the *Albatross*. His confidence grew every hour on board and behind the wheel.

"Captain, I want to thank you, I have learned a lot, I've eaten enough fish and learned the basics. It was time for me to move on; our business is over." Vladimir said.

Chapter 6

Vladimir arrived in Kazan and wasted no time making his way to the Ministry of Agriculture building where months earlier his life changed forever. His jaw tightened and sweat pooled on his forehead. He was fixated on the wooden bench in the center of the courtyard. He jogged away from the bench and stood under the archway of the Ministry; chills flushed over his body at the sight of the wrought iron tree.

Vadimir paced back and forth waiting for Minister Alexandrov to appear. Half past noon, he spotted the Minister pass by the iron tree. Vladimir shuffled up behind him, as they walked down the steps into the courtyard. At the fountain, Vladimir stepped in front of him and stuck his face inches from Alexandrov's own. The Minister's eyes bulged, as he jerked his head back. His red checks flushed white as Vladimir blocked his path. Alexandrov backed up and put a hand out to get distance.

"Do you remember me?" Vladimir said.

"Yes, I do, what are you doing here?" Alexandrov said.

"I am going to be frank with you, sir. You were partly to blame for what happened to me."

"I did not order you to chase down and kill those people."

"You're right. I'm not here to place blame, but you did say. . . at all cost. I'm not here to hurt you; I came to see if you can get me a job in the Ministry. It's the least you should do for me"

There was a long pause. Alexandrov pulled off his shapka and wiped the sweat from his forehead. "I heard you were still in the army."

"I will quit once you give me a job."

"You are poison, I can't do it."

"I have a plan to make a boat load of money, I'll cut you in."

"Private, I doubt you have it in you to make a hundred rubles. Take a hike."

Vladimir's face heated. He moved to within inches of Alexandrov. He covered his mouth. "I understand you have a wife and two young girls. We wouldn't want anything to happen to them, would we?"

"You loser, I have many connections; I'll have you jailed for life, don't screw with me."

"Before I'm caught you will be a widow and have no children. Look Alexandrov, I lost everything in that incident, my family and career are dead. I have nothing to lose!"

Alexandrov's eyes narrowed. His head tilted to the side. I did give you that order... "At all costs." Give me some time to make it happen, you will have to change your last name and work out of a different city. Your name around here is dirt. I can help you with paperwork for the name change. After the paperwork is completed, then you can start working for me in my office in Moscow, I doubt anyone there would recognize you."

"Great, I also want you to get me or buy me an aband-

oned dilapidated whaling ship that is rusting away, docked in Okhotsk."

"That will take some time but should not be a problem," Alexandrov replied.

"I didn't think it would be a problem for you sir."

"Don't be too happy, the job doesn't pay much. What
name would you like to have?" the Minister asked.
Vladimir hesitated for a moment.

"How about Vladimir, Vladimir Diminov."

"See you soon, Vlad."

* * * *

Vladimir had his new identification papers in pocket a
week to the day he arrived in Kazan. He resigned from
the military soon after he received his identity papers.
Vladimir Diminov had his new identity and a new life. His
new job Personal Assistant to the Minister meant
nothing to Vladimir; it was a beginning to an end.

Vladimir's plan was working to perfection. He'd seen
firsthand fishermen making a great living during the
worldwide food shortage. Being a fisherman was not his
goal, though. The work was time consuming and the days
long and hard. He wanted his riches fast and easy. For his
plan to work he needed to make connections from
around the world. The Ministry of Agriculture was the
perfect place to make those connections. The Minister
and his representatives spent a lot of their time traveling
the world trying to solve their food crisis.

Chapter 7

Light snow layered the ground in Moscow, Overcast and fifteen degrees outside, inside not much warmer. He had been assigned a one-room apartment within walking distance to his new office. A wall heater next to the door to the small bathroom worked. The single bed, bowed in the middle with a couple blankets didn't do much. Still one month since returning to Kazan, Vladimir had everything he needed to get rich. He planned on selling his house for cash to facilitate all the parts and supplies needed but the prosecutor general seized his property after the incident in Kazan.

Vladimir did get an advance of salary from Alexandrov and cashed out his savings account. His new crew chipped in funds to help get the operation started. He had a crew working on the newly acquired whaler, that was abandoned and free. The crewmen, all ex-military, most served under him and were discharged after the incident in Kazan, and he made some contacts in Moscow who showed promise. He lay back on his bed day dreaming about his future.

I can't be stopped. No one can stop me. No one! Vladimir dozed off. He didn't sleep long; he never did. He woke drenched in sweat screaming; the same nightmare haunted him. The picture of that day never leaves his mind.

Two beeps sounded, Vladimir sat up and answered...

"Who is it, and why are you calling so late?"

"Vladimir, the old rust bucket is in working order, for how long, well find out. It needs more work, but we are operational; it took a few thousand to fix one of the engines, and we bought five used Zodiacs and all the equipment you requested, for a few thousand more, all your savings is gone. But we're ready; we will work on the second engine in route, only minor issues there."

Vladimir clenched his fist. "Best news I've had in a long, long time."

"See you soon," Dmitri said.

"I have one thing left to do here. I'll see you soon."

* * * *

Vladimir entered Alexandrov's office who sat behind a beautiful cherry wood desk. "Come in Vladimir, how can I help you?"

"Ivan, I want a paid leave for a month. Got personal business to take care of."

Alexandrov eyes narrowed. "What do you mean a leave and paid, you just started working here.?"

Vladimir tilted his head to the side, pointed his finger at Alexandrov. "Look Alexandrov, it's only month, you owe me."

Alexandrov's lips tightened, as he shook his head. "You do realize our country is in dire trouble, people are starving. I need everybody working to help solve this problem."

"Of course, I realize how bad things are. I'll be at our next meeting in Macau."

"This is the last time I can help you; we are all square

after this, Vladimir!"

"Sure Mr. Minister, no problem."

* * * *

Vladimir arrived at the dock in Okhotsk where Dmitri Dyakov and the crew were busy working on the deck equipment. He held the ownership papers above his head, as he boarded the whaler.

"We own this ship men, our ticket to getting rich!" Vladimir yelled. Vladimir scanned the deck on his way to the wheelhouse, inspecting the work the crew completed. He found Dmitri in the wheelhouse wiring up a loud speaker.

"The helm looks good," Vladimir said. "How is the engine running?"

"Engine in good shape; we are ready and eager to go," Dmitri said.

Vladimir stared out the window, surveyed down onto the deck. "Are the winches and Zodiacs in working order?"

Dmitri stood tall. "All good and the butchers are ready to slice and dice."

"Let's get rich. Tell the men to remove the dock lines."

Vladimir started up the engines and eased the old whaler away from the dock, as the last dock line was removed. He called the crew to the wheelhouse once the whaler hit open water.

Sitting tall in the captain's chair, he said, "Men, we're heading for a remote beach on the Oregon coast of America. The U.S military and Coast Guard are depleted. We need to take advantage of this fact before they realize what we are doing. We have an opportunity for great wealth," Vladimir said.

A roar from the crew echoed in the wheelhouse, as they dispersed. "Nobody can stop us – nobody!" Vladimir screamed.

Chapter 8

Bandon, Oregon

They arrived at the remote beach south of the Shell Islands for the seal rescue and cleanup before sun up. Jacob and Xian unloaded all their equipment and boxes of heavy-duty garbage bags. The bone chilling wind kidnapped sand from the towering dunes and propelled thousands of painful sand needles into their faces. Han being out front took the most abuse. Jacob and Xian followed close behind. Their heads down as they struggled through the loose sand.

They stopped and rested just before the peak on the last dune before the beach to escape the numbing wind and sand. Jacob noticed strange noises from the direction of the beach. "Sounds like motorboats in the distance."

"The seal herds are unusually loud this morning," Xian said.

Han crested the dune first. Jacob's foot sunk into the sand as he topped the dune a step behind her. Jacob's body tensed. The light from the moon illuminated the silhouette of three men, one walking toward them a hundred feet away. Jacob stopped in his tracks, sinking in the soft sand. They carried long guns.

"What in God's name?" Jacob whispered. Han had not yet seen the man. Jacob dove on her and brought her to the ground, covered her mouth before she verbally abused him. He pointed to the dark figure and released his hand. Han's heart pounded through her back into his chest as the man walked toward them. Jacob held his hand out, signaling Xian to stop. Xian had seen the man and ducked for cover behind a mound of sand and ice plant. They were directly in his path.

"Dig into the sand, Han," Jacob whispered.

They squirmed as deep into the sand and beach grass as possible. Jacob hoped the light of the moon did not give them away.

One man marched to within a few feet of Jacob and scanned all directions, he turned and walked back toward the beach.

Jacob and Han laid there for minutes in silence; Han's heart still pounded into his chest.

Xian crawled up to them, his face covered in sand. "What the heck was that all about?" he whispered, while wiping his face.

Jacob pushed to his knees and peered over the grass.

"It looks like they are patrolling the dunes, stay down they might be back. They are not American, foreign accent,"

"It was Russian, Jacob, for sure it was Russian," Han said.

"Stay down and follow me, I need to take a look and see what is going on down there," Jacob said.

Jacob led them a few yards to the top of the dune and peered down onto the beach. Jacob's jaw clenched tight, he grasped a handful of sand and crushed it, before tossing the molded clump to the ground.

"It looks like an army down there. They are using Zodiac boats; they look like bees hovering around a hive," Jacob said.

"Do you see that large ship off shore? Xian said.

"That is a whaling ship; see the long ramp at the rear?" Jacob said.

The men on shore with cow prods were herding the seals away from the water while men in the Zodiacs drove the seal back toward the beach. A steel net was deployed a few feet from shore. It stopped any seal from escape. The seals were corralled, cut off from escape, and men with shot guns unloaded one slug into the head. The dead seals were run through with round steel rods, one through the shoulder the other through the lower back then connected to a long steel cable with floats attached every few feet. Hundreds of seals were attached to the one cable that ran all the way out to the whaling ship. Large wheels wound the steel cable pulling the seals out to the ship and up the ramp at the stern. Some of the seals still alive, pummeled the surf trying to escape.

"I can't believe what's happening, am I in a dream or what?" Han said.

"What can we do?" Xian said.

Jacob's teeth ground, his lip curled up.

There was nothing to do, except lay there in the sand and watch as these killers decimated the entire herd on the beach. The three stared in disgust at the butchery until it was over. With the beach depleted of animals, the ship disappeared into the darkness of the Pacific.

Jacob stood up on top of the sand dune glaring into the

Pacific. Sand blistered his face, his heart pounded. He didn't care. Jacob found it difficult to move, powerless like no other time in his life. As daylight trickled over the horizon, it illuminated a blood-stained beach and burgundy-colored waves crashing onto shore. A blood tide pushed the bloody water, deep onto the beach.

Xian was shaking his head and mumbling. Han had covered her mouth and stared at the red ghosted beach.

"This is sickening, I want to hurt somebody right now," Jacob said.

"The seal rescue and beach cleanup seems meaningless now, the only thing left on the beach, bloody water and dead jellies," Xian said.

A shiver shot up Jacob's spine. "Anybody bring your cell phone?"

"No, didn't want it getting wet," Xian said.

"What the hell did we just witness?" Han asked.

"Poachers, Russian poachers," Jacob shouted.

"I have to call headquarters" Xian muttered.

"Yeah, I will try Fish and Game, maybe they will have someone in the area," Jacob said.

"The world has gone crazy, how can something like this happen?" Han said.

"It starts with a defective U.S. government defaulting. Now there are only two Coast Guard boats patrolling the entire West Coast and Alaska. Fish and Game does not exist for each state anymore, it's per region, and there aren't enough officers left to patrol. The Navy had deep cuts, it's nonexistent in this area most of the year." Jacob said.

"Things might spiral out of control fast," Xian said.

"Things are out of control," Han said.

"Yeah, the more I think about it, the more sense it makes. The entire Northern Hemisphere, including Russia and China, is in a long, severe drought. Food production is so low people are starving to death in many countries. Throw in the fact that China had that nuclear issue and catastrophic flood one year destroying major infrastructure. In the U.S., we keep hiring corrupt politicians with no convictions for the country, except to gain power and suck what they can out of it." Jacob's face flushed. "The results are a leaderless ship sailing in circles. That is how it starts, Xian."

Xian cleared his throat "Wow, hopeless."

Chapter 9

Jacob arrived at Joe's Coffee earlier than usual, eager to hear the test results from the labs at INECE. Xian and Han were late as usual. Jacob sat at the table next to the front door, a dirt infused window obscured the view of the parking lot, his cup drained.

"Joe, how about a refill?"

"Coming right up, sorry about the delay, Stacy called in sick today."

Jacob started on his second cup as Xian and Han walked through the door. "As usual, right-on time," Jacob said.

"Han's fault," Xian said.

Han's eyes cut through Xian like a razor.

"What is the damage from the test results Xian?" Jacob said.

"No luck on the poachers," Xian said.

Jacob shook his head. "Doesn't surprise me."

"I do have information on the die off. The fish and birds died from eating small pieces of the plastic; it blocked their digestive tracts. Wildlife caught in the nets, fishing line, and the plastic speaks for itself. Low levels of radiation may have something to do with Cyanea Capillata."

"You're kidding, radiation?" Jacob said.

"They think it's possible that the radiation from the nuclear meltdown may have contributed," Xian said.

"Unbelievable," Han said.

Jacob pulled his hat off. "What about the jellies?

"The jellies are a more difficult to determine; they think a change in the ocean temperature due to pollution, maybe a stronger current with a direction change, even very low levels of radiation, and other pollution," Xian said. "All might have had an effect."

Jacob downed the last of his coffee. "Man, we're in some deep trouble."

"Not good," Han said.

"What's next for you guys?" Jacob said.

"Our next assignment is in Vietnam, taking on the illegal shark fin trade. It involves some risky undercover work, by Han," Xian said.

"Han, you volunteered, didn't you?" Jacob said.

"Yeah, it's in Vietnam. Only makes sense," Han said. "How about you, Jacob?"

"After all that's been going on, I don't think I have a choice. I'll take a trip to Portland, and check in with INECE and see about a job. I wish both of you, God speed. Keep in touch."

"Will do," Xian said. "The job is yours Jacob, I guarantee."

Chapter 10

The lights of Port Vostochny meant money to Vladimir; they scored on a valuable commodity and were a short distance away from putting money in their pockets, and where Vladimir would make contact with buyers from Portland and Seattle for his next payday. The butchered seal meat was about to be delivered. Vladimir's first big score was almost complete. His pride dripped out of his mouth.

"I am a genius. No one can stop me. Never again will I be someone's doormat." Vladimir screamed.

A half a mile from the docks, Yuri burst into the wheelhouse, gasping for air in a panic. "One engine is smoking, the other shut down, we are going to lose control!"

Vladimir slammed his fist into the side window. "Damn this rust bucket!" He shut down the engines, shaking his head. "Go tell Dmitri to set the anchors, I will meet you in the engine room."

The old whaler dragged the anchors for one hundred feet before it stopped a mile from port. Vladimir sprinted below deck. The smoke was thick as he entered the engine room. His eyes burned. "What the hell is the damage, Yuri?"

"One engine needs a valve job, maybe more work, the other needs a head gasket," Yuri grumbled. "They are seventy to eighty years old, what you expect?"

"Son of a bitch," Vladimir slammed his fist on the tool

bench. "This is going to eat into our profits. Engines aren't cheap to fix or buy. Our next operation is on hold until we fix the engines. I will send you some help once I get to shore. You and Dmitri get this rust bucket to port and off load the product; we need to get paid. Keep me informed about the cost to fix this ancient motors. I have a meeting to attend to in Macau. Big money in China for our next score."

"I hope we can find parts for this old ship," Yuri said.

"Buy or steal the parts if you have to. Do whatever it takes."

"This might take weeks, longer if we find more damage," Yuri said.

Vladimir's face flushed red; he jabbed a finger in Yuri's face. "Just get it done. I'll work on plan B,"

* * * *

Sweat beaded on Vladimir's forehead, as he stepped off the plane in Macau. He met Alexandrov and the rest of the Russian delegation in the lobby of the Macau Marriot.

"Three days of meetings and then you are done Vladimir," Minister Alexandrov said. "Three boring days of meetings you mean."

The Russians, Chinese and all of Asia searched for answers to the region's food shortages. Vladimir's job was to sit behind Minister Alexandrov and take notes. Vladimir spent most of his time studying his counterparts. There had to be someone there desperate enough to join him.

After the daily meetings, Vladimir walked the docks studying the different fishing vessels. At the end of the docks a business stood out, a sign above the door with green lights flashing pulled him in. He received some stern looks and raised eyebrows as he bellied up to the bar and ordered in Mandarin his usual, a shot of Russian vodka. Vladimir had learned some Mandarin while he trained with the Chinese military after the war, just enough to make small talk. He raised his glass, but before he tossed it down, a skinny Asian man in a suit and tie, thick black glasses sat next to him. "I hear you been inquiring about fins?"

"Who are you? What do you care?"

The Asian man covered his mouth. "My name is Qian and that depends what you're looking for."

Vladimir tilted his head to the side. "Who do you work for? and what do you want?"

"I hear you been asking questions around the docks. Maybe I can help in your desire to acquire or sell?"

"How can you?"

Qian leaned back, pushed his glasses tight to the bridge of his nose, crossed his arms. "Let's just say I'm in sales."

"Big money in food right now. A lot of money being made off seal meat."

"Seal meat?" Qian, rubbed his forehead. "Interesting,"

Vladimir leaned forward. "Maybe we can work something out," Vladimir said in a low mono tone voice. "Give me a contact number, I'll be in touch."

Vladimir's confidence grew; with the exception of the old rust bucket, things were working to perfection. He had buyers from America and maybe this guy in China.

Shark fins in the South China Sea would be his biggest money maker to date, if he pulled it off.

Vladimir's restlessness and hunger for riches moved him off the rust bucket. He had another plan. The chaos around the world would give him an advantage to win now. Waiting for the repair of the rust bucket was no longer an option; it might be a month until it got fixed. He needed a boat and crew now; riches do not wait for the weak. His profits might dry up fast fixing the engines for the old whaler. Plan B steered him to a location in the South China Sea, specifically Malaysian Borneo area near Layang. Hammerhead sharks had been known to feed in large schools there.

Vladimir made sure he arrived at the docks before sunrise. He was looking for his next victim. The docks were full of activity; some crewmen loaded supplies while others waited on the docks looking for work. *I'll bet half the boats docked here have hunted sharks before. It should not be hard to find a crew.* Vladimir still needed a boat. He marched down the entire docks, but did not find a boat to charter or steal, he had to go another route. He spied out a couple of gillnetters and trawlers. He planned on selling the whole shark unlike these criminals who just cut off the fins and dump the shark back into the water to die. Vladimir's goal was two hundred hammerheads. The hammerhead sharks did travel in large schools; he would try going after them first. Netting was the best way to get a large catch fast. Vladimir's idea was to attract a large school, but chumming would not attract the large numbers in a small area he needed for the big quick haul. His brilliant idea came to him while walking the docks in Okhotsk – bait balls. Three or four live bait balls would work if done right.

Word around the dock sent Vladimir to one captain and crew in particular – the *Majestic Netter*, captained by Ting Hu. Vladimir leaned against the pier post and spied the boat from a distance. Studying every movement of the crew. One man walked the deck, barking out orders, seemed to be the one in charge, Vladimir studied him, before stopping in front of the *Majestic Netter*,

"I need to speak to the captain!" Vladimir yelled,

"You're looking at him, what do you want?"

"I'm looking for a spot on your boat," Vladimir said.

"Come aboard,"

Vladimir was ready with a couple of stories, anything to get aboard. He approached the man on deck. The apparent captain was a short man, an untrimmed beard with a long pony tail, a hard-looking man with a sunburned wrinkled face. The hat he wore flopped to one side, like a fifty-year-old sock.

Word around the dock, the man was shady.

"My name is Vladimir, are you looking for a deck hand?"

"Not really, definitely not someone who looks like you. The man pulled on his beard. What experience do you have?"

"Experienced in long line fishing."

"We only Trawl. Net fishing. I only hire a seasoned reliable hand for cheap."

"I've fished in the Sea of Okhotsk, Russia."

"How long?

"More than a year."

"Not good enough, my friend. Try someone else down the docks."

"Sir. What is your name?" Vladimir said.

"Ting Hu, captain of this ship, not that it's any of your business."

"Captain, how 'bout I pay you to teach me the ropes about netting? I am buying a boat similar to yours, and I need the experience trawling. I will pay you two thousand."

Hu turned his head toward the sea, hesitated for a minute, and eyed Vladimir. "Three thousand and you got a deal."

Vladimir hesitated; he didn't want to seem too anxious. "Ok, three it is." Vladimir lowered his hat. *Hook line and sinker.*

"Be at the dock at 4:30 tomorrow morning; we are heading out to sea at five," Captain Hu said.

"Where are we going to fish?"

"The South China Sea, then down toward Malaysia."

Vladimir walked down the uneven wooden dock his chest thrust out, shoulders back. This is perfect. He turned toward the *Majestic Netter. I am an unstoppable genius.*

He stepped off the docks onto solid ground and immediately called Yuri with the good news.

"Yuri, I found a boat," Vladimir said.

"Great, we will have the rust bucket running sooner rather than later; found all the parts we need, the one engine was just a blown head gasket, easy fix." Yuri said.

"If everything goes as planned, I will meet you at our planned location off the coast of Vietnam. Talk to you soon."

Chapter 11

The morning was cool, the sky full of thunderous clouds reaching the heavens. The docks were quiet except for one ship. Vladimir's boots clicked loud all the way down the wooden docks to the ship, announcing his presence. He noticed the deck hands loading supplies onto the *Majestic Netter* as he approached. He counted six crew members plus Hu from the dock.

The freezer trawler was not more than a couple years old. Vladimir wrestled with, how someone like Ting Hu had a ship like this. He was an independent fisherman, and a ship like this usually was owned by a corporation or the CCP.

Hu stood on the deck eyeing Vladimir making his way up the ramp. "Stop right there, before you board, I have to tell you, the price has gone up."

Vladimir knew many criminals like Hu, it was expected.

"What? How much more?"

"The new price is five thousand."

"How about four thousand?"

"Five thousand, take it or leave."

Vladimir shook his head as he boarded. "You're killing me Captain, five it is."

Vladimir knew he would get it all back. Pulling the money out of his backpack, he noticed Hu's eyes flatten. Vladimir had seen that look of evil a time or two. With money in hand, Hu's stiff posture loosened, his hard glare turned to a smile.

Vladimir knew he had the right ship soon after talking to Hu. The equipment on board was everything he needed to complete his plan. There were two types of nets – the encircling nets and Purse Seine needed for catching sardines or other bait fish and the larger nets used for bigger fish. Vladimir assumed if all went as planned Hu and his crew would do all the work catching the bait fish then his crew would be ready to take over from there.

"First Mate Fan will show you around and where to store your gear," Hu said.

Vladimir stored his gear on a bunk and followed the crewmen for a walk around. The ship was even better than he had hoped; besides the netting he needed, it had tanks to store live bait and refrigeration to keep the catch fresh. He ended the tour in the helm where Hu was steering the ship past the sea wall at a snail pace. Hu nodded at Vladimir as he entered the wheelhouse.

"The first day I want you to just watch my men, don't touch anything unless they ask, you understand," Hu said.

"Ok, Captain."

"Two days out to sea, we will be at the Paracel Islands west of Vietnam, fishing for sardines or silver fish."

Vladimir's lips tightened. *Things are going as planned and Yuri will be in that area.*

Hu tapped Vladimir on the shoulder. "If I catch enough, I will sell whatever we don't need for a nice dollar in

Vietnam."

Vladimir did not trust Hu or his shady crew. He detected eyes watching as he strolled around the boat, expecting to stare down a blade. Vladimir was confident they would not get over on him; they had no idea the kind of hell that was about to come down on them.

Vladimir wandered away alone while the crew worked. He searched for weapons, radios or anything that would help them and cause him trouble after he made his move. He noticed two cell phones lying on bunks in the crew room and one ship-to-shore radio in the helm. Hu had his own cell phone laid out on the dash.

The first day out to sea, Vladimir spent most of his time searching for guns and pretending to look interested in what the crew was doing. He searched the whole ship, except the captain's quarters, a locked cabinet in the hallway by the helm and the cabinet in the wheelhouse. Vladimir would wait for the right time to search Hu's quarters.

Looking around the boat, Vladimir wondered how Hu owned this beautiful new Trawler; it was above and beyond what any other fisherman had at the docks. Word on the docks was Hu would do anything for a buck. Vladimir had no doubt Hu earned his money by illegal activities. He had an idea it might be shark fins. Vladimir shook his head. *He is stealing money out of my pocket. Not for long Hu.*

The second day out to sea, the *Majestic Netter* passed the Spratly Islands heading south. The orange sun peeked over the horizon, a warm light breeze from the west showered the ship.

Vladimir sat in the only private spot on the trawler – the commode. He heard commotion on deck, looking out the window he spotted the Islands, a perfect time to call Yuri on the satellite phone...

"Yuri come in, you there, come in," Vladimir said.

"I hear you, Vladimir."

"Where are you?"

"I have one engine working. We are on our way to refuel in Quy Nhon Port."

"We are starting to fish near the Spratly Islands. The captain said if they caught extra bait fish they would sell them in Da Nang Port tonight. Be ready to go."

"We'll be ready, Vladimir. We have the fine netting we need to simulate a bait balls."

"Ok, the bait balls will draw in a lot of sharks; I'll call you later, over and out."

Three loud *thuds* vibrated on the commode door. Vladimir's heart thumped hard into his chest, his eyes widened and forehead wrinkled.

"If you want to learn, you might want to come topside. We're setting net now, Fan said."

"Be right there." Wow *close call, did he hear?*

Vladimir eased the door open, expecting a shiv to the chest. He slammed the door all the way open. No crewmen stood guard over him. He took a deep breath.

Topside Vladimir watched as Hu's crewmen unloaded a small seven-foot aluminum boat into the water with two men onboard. One drove while the other held on to the main line of the net as they drove the skiff into a circle around the bait fish, the net rolled off with precision. The men circled back around to the trawler where they handed off the main line.

"How many times are we going to set this net?" Vladimir asked a deck hand at the stern.

"Depends on the haul size – you dumb or something?" the deck hand said while attaching the main line to the drum.

Vladimir shrugged. *This fool has no idea.* Vladimir watched close as they set the net, studying every task of each man. They were efficient, as every man performed his duties without hesitation. Within a short time, they rolled the net in loaded with sardines. The men pumped the first haul into one tank. Hours later, they pumped the last net full of sardines into the live bait tank full of sea water. The tanks were overflowing with fish. Vladimir made his way to the helm and sat beside Hu.

"Why the need for so many bait fish?" Vladimir said.

Hu stood behind the wheel with a big grin on his face. "You'll see soon."

"What's next, Captain?"

"Were going to Vietnam, sell some of today's catch, then fun in Da Nang Port City, ok with you, Vladimir?"

"Yeah, sounds good to me."

Vladimir had a wide grin, as he strutted down to his bunk dripping with pride. He dreamed about this moment for a long time but didn't expect his dream to include this beautiful trawler.

The sun was just starting to set, as Hu motored into the port. Vladimir stayed in the helm learning everything about the operation of the trawler as possible.

"Where are we going tomorrow, Hu?"

Hu was hesitant to say at first. "We stay in city one night then head south toward Malaysia early morning. You will see a lot tomorrow, learn much, even how to pilot ship,"

"That is what I was hoping for, Hu!" *Piloting this ship would be a piece of cake compared to the rust bucket. Working Hu over has been easy.*

* * * *

Hu docked the trawler into position without incident. The crew had the buoys set and the trawler tied off with the three-strand nylon lines in no time. An hour later, the partially frozen sardines were hoisted off. Vladimir was impressed with the precision of Hu's crew. The buyer paid Hu after the last load hit the scales. Hu called his crew to the galley over the loudspeaker.

"We are going to dock here for the night, all you go into town tonight and celebrate the big catch; everybody makes money today," Hu said. "There are cheap taxis to take you to a local hotel and a night club across the street from the hotel, caters to fishermen, just be back by five, tomorrow morning."

"Hu, I have no reason to go in to the city; I am going to stay on the ship tonight," Vladimir said to him.

"Nobody stays on ship tonight, you can't stay here alone, you must go."

Vladimir shook his head as he turned away. He had no choice. Hu handed out spending money to all, even Vladimir. The crew gathered their bags and ran off the ship to the dock. Vladimir picked up his backpack and started for the taxis waiting on the dock.

Vladimir's fist tightened, as he peered out the taxi window, he wanted to inflict pain on Hu.

"Where are we going, how long of a ride?"

"Don't worry, have fun, fifteen minutes north of here, hotel and club called Little Miss Saigon. It's a place where all fishermen go."

Vladimir imagined the type of club it was, dubious no doubt. They crossed an old wooden bridge a mile from the dock. The look of the modern city started to change. The buildings were old and run down. Street people were congregating up and down the narrow street, selling everything from food to jewelry out of two wheeled carts. Mopeds, the main form of transportation raced up and down the street.

The taxi stopped in front of an oddly painted rundown motel – *this does not look good.* The front doors were open. A fan on the ceiling rotated as fast as the second hand of his watch. The clerk at the front desk was a thin man with no hair and round glasses.

"Sixty a night," the clerk said. In English

"How did you know I spoke English? Vladimir said.

"You look like you speak English. Room twelve, top of the stairs."

Vladimir turned to the crewmen behind him. "I take it the club across the street is the place to go,"

"We'll meet you there later tonight."

The stairs creaked and bowed with every step. Vladimir opened the paper-thin door to his room at the end of the hall. The single bed and chair filled the rank room. He stepped sideways to reach the window; it overlooked the street and the night club. The bathroom down the hall said it all, the fragrance made itself distinguished in Vladimir's room. Vladimir sunk into the soft bed, staring at the orange paint peeling from the ceiling. His eyes closed, as he dozed off.

Chapter 12

Loud music woke Vladimir. A large crowd congergated outside the club. He wasn't really interested in the club but went there to gather information from his new-found shipmates, while they were drunk. He pushed through the crowd and dropped into a seat at the bar, tossed his pack under his chair, and ordered Russian vodka over ice.

Looking around the club, he noticed a few young women in skimpy dresses. Within five minutes, three young Vietnamese women had approached him for a dance, but each time he declined. Vladimir downed his vodka, scanned the bar looking for his shipmates, none were there. He wondered if they went somewhere else or were still at the hotel. Something didn't feel right. He took a deep breath, as his heart skipped. He went outside and didn't see any crew. He hustled back to the hotel. The clerk sat behind the bamboo framed counter, watching TV.

"Have you seen my shipmates?" Vladimir asked.

"They left in a taxi not long after you checked in. The taxi driver is parked outside the hotel waiting for a fare if you want to ask him where they went."

Vladimir's eyes narrowed; he gave a nod.

The taxi driver was leaning on the hood of his car smoking. Vladimir punched through the hotel door.

"Did you have a fare with six Chinese men from the hotel today?" Vladimir said.

"To harbor, why you ask?"

Vladimir rolled his head back and let out a scream. Vladimir's head dropped; his eyes closed. "Take me to the harbor now, make it fast."

Vladimir slammed the door, and the taxi sped off toward the harbor. He opened his backpack to call Yuri. "What the hell?" he tore through the pack, opened every zipper, and found nothing. The money was gone, a rolled-up newspaper with a smiling face drawn on it, was left in its place. He searched deeper into the pack for the SAT phone, nothing but a rotted piece of wood with the word "fool" carved into it.

"That son of a bitch! Damm him!" Vladimir screamed.

The driver slammed on the brakes. "What's wrong?"

"I've been ripped off; my money, passport and phone are gone. Get me to the docks fast."

Hu will pay for this. Sneaky bastards must have snuck into my room while I was sleeping.

"Can you go any faster?" Vladimir said.

"Not if you want to get there in one piece."

* * * *

Vladimir jerked his head back as they pulled into the harbor, he took a deep breath, staring at the empty dock. The *Majestic Netter* was gone.

That bastard. I knew he was a hard-core criminal. What now? Money gone and no phone. Vladimir pressed his hand against his forehead. "Driver, do you have a cell phone I can use?"

"Yes, but you must pay the fare first."

"Here's your money, give me the phone."

Vladimir's call to Yuri went to voicemail. "Damn it, Yuri!" Vladimir punched the back seat. "Call me at the hotel named...Little Miss Saigon, Liberty Da Nang Port city once you get this message." Vladimir rubbed his brow and mumbled all the way back to the hotel.

He pushed through the hotel door. The clerk hadn't moved, still watching the old black and white TV, the antenna spread wide. He started up the stairs toward his room. "Hey, come and get me right away if a call comes in for me," Vladimir yelled to the hotel clerk. "If I am not in my room, I'll be at the club across the street."

The clerk never moved but gave a thumbs up.

Vladimir paced the small bedroom, his mind racing, planning his revenge. Passing by the open window, his attention turned to the club across the street. *Vodka, I need vodka.*

* * * *

Vladimir sat at the table next to the bar. Two girls kept asking him to dance; he ignored them. His mind stuck on a way out of hell, he downed a shot and ordered another. He noticed two beautiful Vietnamese women sitting at the next table eyeing him.

"Hello ladies, can I buy you a drink?"

"Not now, thank you."

Eavesdropping, he overheard the name Han; she sounded like the one in charge of the club. He was good at manipulation. He sent two drinks to their table hoping to start a conversation. They did not send them back. Vladimir shuffled his chair over to their table.

"Hi my name is Vladimir, what's yours?"

"I'm Han, this is Kim."

"What's your job here, Han?"

Han pushed her hair out of her eyes. "My family owns this club."

Kim shuffled her chair closer to him. "Do you want to dance? What do you do for a living?"

"I am in international trade."

"Why are you here in Vietnam?" Han said.

"It's a long story, would you like to hear?" Before she answered... "I wanted to start my own fishing business; I paid a captain of a trawler from China to teach me the ropes. He stole all my money, phone, and passport then left me here."

"Have you called the police?" Kim said.

"Yeah, they said they will look into it. I just don't have the time to wait. I have to track them myself somehow. I have an idea where they are going. My friends have a ship in the Quy Nhon, can you help me get there?"

"You can get there by air, train, car or by boat," Han said.

"I have no money with me or a passport. Once I see my friends in Quy Nhon, money will not be a problem. I'll pay you cash."

"Let me make some calls and see if we can help you. It won't be cheap." Han bit her lip, lifted up two fingers. "Two thousand U.S."

"No problem."

* * * *

Han's heart raced, she jumped two stairs at a time, onto the top landing, and ran down the narrow hall into the office and dialed. Three long agonizing rings.

"Hello Han, this better be good news."

"I think we finally might have him."

"Have who?"

"The Russian, Vladimir! He is here and asked me for help, can you believe it?"

"You're joking, how can you be sure it's him?"

"He matches the description and picture you sent me of the Russian you met in China. He said he'd been ripped off by a Chinese fisherman and was abandoned here. He wants help getting to his friends on a ship at Quy Nhon so he can track down the captain who ripped him off."

"We need to keep him there until I can get a boat a crew to follow him. I need to catch them in the act. Stall him anyway you can."

"He doesn't have money or a passport. I have an idea – my uncle has a boat docked here; if I can convince him that my uncle's boat is the only way for him to get to his friends, we can stall him."

"Han, this will be dangerous. Are you sure you want to involve your uncle?"

"I'll call him and see if he is ok with it."

"Ok, what does uncle's boat look like?"

"It has a wooden hull painted red, and the wheelhouse is painted green, and a yellow flag with a fish painted black on it."

"Han, be careful, this guy is dangerous. If we do this right, we can get this degenerate."

I will call my uncle right now. Han did not hesitate; she dialed her uncle the second she hung up. Five rings....

"Uncle, this is your niece, Han."

"Han hello, been too long, how are you?" Uncle Yang said.

"Great, I need some help."

"Whatever my niece needs I will do."

"I need a boat ride over to the Quy Nhon."

"Quy Nhon, no problem. I planned on fishing in that area today. I'll be here waiting."

Han sat down next to Vladimir. "I have an uncle with a boat. He will take you for the two thousand.

"I will meet you in front of the hotel; I need to check with the clerk about a phone call," Vladimir said.

Han and Kim remained at the table.

"Who is this guy that you would go out of your way to help him?" Kim said.

"Xian and I have been trying to arrest this guy for poaching for a long time., We believe he has been poaching all around the world. I can't believe he fell into our lap today. I don't think he suspects anything. This club is finally starting to pay off. Not only are we catching criminals selling shark fins, we might just catch a big fish soon."

* * * *

Vladimir sat on the hotel steps, as Han pulled up. She unlocked the passenger door of her old four-door Toyota.

"I will get you there as quick as possible."

"I am grateful, thanks."

Han raced through old town toward the port.

"Can I borrow your cell phone? I need to make a call?" Vladimir asked.

"Sure, help yourself."

"Can we drive directly to Cai Mep?"

Han hesitated. "It's a dangerous drive; I would not feel comfortable driving on the road, many carjackings. My uncle is waiting for us at Saigon Port; it won't be long and Cai Mep is only a couple hour boat ride."

Vladimir shook his head, as he dialed Yuri's number. It rang once.

"Yuri, it's Vladimir, did you get my message?"

"Yeah."

"I am on my way to you now, I'll be there in a couple of hours."

"One engine is working fine, we are working on the other, a couple of days to repair it."

"Han, can you pull the car over, I want to talk to my friend in private." Han drove to a dirt patch a few feet off the pavement and skidded to a stop. Vladimir jumped out of the car slamming the door behind him. "Damn, Yuri, can't you guys get it right? I would call this operation off if there wasn't so much potential profit. I have to go after this Hu character now or I'll never catch up to him."

"We are doing everything we can to fix the second engine, running on one old engine probably will not last long, we need both," Yuri said.

"Ok, be ready for a takeover. I'll see you soon; my ride says a couple of hours."

* * * *

Han and Vladimir arrived at Da Nang port just before sun up. A dense fog covered the port. A few lights dimly illuminated the docks. One boat with all its lights on stood out. Han spotted her uncle right away. He was busy cleaning the windshield.

"Hello Uncle!" Han yelled.

Uncle Jang waved at them. She spoke a few words in Vietnamese to her uncle, explaining the plan. He nodded.

"Vladimir, my uncle does not speak English or Russian, so I will be coming along." *No way I was going to leave my uncle alone with this criminal.*

"Your English is really good, where did you learn it?"

"America, went to school there," Han said. "Where did you learn English?"

"I have American relatives, learned from them. I have no problem with you coming along, can we hurry?"

"Uncle, can we go now"? Han spoke.

"Once engine is warm," Jang replied.

Uncle Jang's traditional fishing boat motored south through the dense fog at a good pace.

Jang idled his fishing boat into the port of Cai Mep. Vladimir stood on the bow barking out the directions. "Over there next to that whaling ship."

Jang passed the stern of the massive whaling ship, a long ramp at the stern led up to the deck of the whaler. He took his cap off and shook his head, wiped sweat from his brow. "This close enough?" he said.

"Perfect," Vladimir said.

Four men from the whaler stood on the dock as Jang pulled in. Vladimir jumped onto the dock with the docking line in hand. He said a few words to the men and tied off. Two men jumped into the boat, pushing and shoving Han and Jang into the helm.

"What the hell is going on here, Vladimir?" Han shouted.

The short stocky man rapped up Han in a bear hug and put to her knees, the skinny bearded man put a head lock on Jang and wrangled him to the deck, without a struggle.

"You son of a bitch Vladimir," Han screamed. Before being gagged and tied up.

"I need your boat; stay calm and you won't be hurt," Vladimir said.

Han kicked and screamed through the gag as the four men carried Her and Jang into the whaler.

"Do you want someone to go with you?" Yuri asked.

"No, I got this," Vladimir raised his AK74 into the air as he drove away. "I won't be beaten by this double-crosser!"

Vladimir checked Jang's fuel and set course for the Spratly Islands. Hu had a couple of hours head start, but Vladimir had one advantage. Hu had no idea what kind of hell was about to descend on him.

Vladimir left the port at full speed, leaving a trail of black smoke. The bow of Jang's boat slammed into the swells for hours with no sighting of Hu. Vladimir headed straight for the Spratly Islands; the area Hu had caught the bait fish.

Hours after leaving port, Vladimir made his first sighting of life, a vessel west of the Spratly islands. It had a similar size and look to that of Hu's boat. Vladimir drove closer but not too close. He circled away, not wanting to draw attention. As he moved away, he noticed buoys floating in a large circle with familiar markings.

Chapter 13

Xian idled into the harbor before sunrise at Cai Mep. The ten-meter patrol boat was a mono-hull deep V-step glider capable of 55 knots, a range of 250 nautical miles with a turret bridge on top of the wheelhouse and a .50 caliber machine gun on the bow. They searched the port for an hour and did not see any sign of Han or Jang.

Xian, paced from stern to bow, sweeping his hand through his hair, waiting for a call from Han.

No call came. Xian was anxious, he had to call her. The phone rang four times before it was answered.

"Hello," a deep-throated voice answered.

Xian scratched the back of his head with his pinky finger hearing the voice. "Who is this? Where is Han?" There was no answer.

Xian knew Han was in trouble. He recognized Vladimir's voice. He called his crew to the wheelhouse. "Han is in trouble, men. Keep an eye out for a small traditional fishing boat painted red and green, probably six meters in length."

They searched every slip in port and found nothing, no boat, no Han. They tied off to an empty slip. Xian's mouth tightened; brow raised. He had regret letting Han take on this dangerous task. He gazed out to sea and rubbed his forehead.

"What now, Xian?" Bo said.

"Set course due west, I'll call headquarters," Xian stepped down into his captain's quarters to make the call...

"Hello Xian, what's going on?" Supervisor Kang said.

"Boss, I need Han's cell phone traced, she is in trouble, can you, do it?"

"We will try."

"Vladimir may have figured out our undercover- op. I have to find her fast."

"I told you not to let her get too deep into this operation. Why didn't you listen?"

"She was just supposed to drop him off."

"I hope this doesn't blow up on you. Careers and lives are on the line."

"Understood."

"Where is he going?"

"Han told me he is after a fisherman with a trawler."

"If we find the fisherman, we will find them both. What are they fishing for?"

"If he ripped off Vladimir, he is dirty, doing something illegal. Maybe shark."

"If it's shark fins, our information has determined the general location of where to start looking."

"We will head north, to the Paracel Islands," Xian said.

"I will contact all coastguard operators in the area and see if we can get help. Call me if you need anything, I'll call you if we find the location of Han's phone."

"I think their fishing for sharks, maybe around the Paracel Islands," Xian said.

Xian gathered the crew together in the wheelhouse. "We're headed toward the Paracel Islands looking for a trawler or a red and green fishing boat. Be alert."

"Xian, who are these people we are going after?" Bo said.

"We have been working to get this Russian the day we started working for AECEN. He is reckless and greedy and would sell his soul for money; his greed is what will allow us to take him down."

"The South China Sea is over a million square miles. We can't do this alone; we need help." Bo said.

"Maybe a close friend will help... Jacob," Xian said.

"How can he help?" Bo said.

"He was in the U.S. Coast Guard. Maybe he has some connections with the Philippines or Taiwan coast guard."

Chapter 14

Vladimir was at sea for hours. Jang's fishing boat was being tossed around like a toy. The helm swayed and cracked as each swell pounded the bow. Vladimir gripped the wheel tight, his knuckles turning white. Buckets of water washed over the bow, flooding the helm, soaking his boots up to his ankles. The bow plunged deep into each swell, taking on more and more water. Vladimir briefly spotted floats in the water, before the boat dropped down and his vision was impaired. The waves were relentless, Vladimir white knuckled the wheel tight, wind and waves crashing onto the deck was deafening, he heard a faint ping from his phone, the call he was waiting for...

"We are on our way," Yuri said.

"Great timing Yuri. I found Hu's net. The markings on the floats gave him away. Steer due west to the Spratly Islands, you can't miss him, he is the only one out there, you will see his lights."

"Roger that, Vladimir," Yuri said.

Before Vladimir pulled away, he noticed a lot of thrashing in the net.

Vladimir left the net and headed away, just far enough to keep in visual contact of the floats. He put out a pole to make it look like he was fishing. Two hours later he received a call from Yuri.

"How far from the Spratly Islands are you?" Yuri said.

"A few miles out on the northern end. Keep going northwest; you'll see us soon. I've got him in my sights."

"What's your plan?"

"He's fishing for sharks; we will let him do all the work then I take everything tonight."

"What are we going to do with the old man and the girl?"

"Keep them tied up below deck and don't let them see anything. We'll let them go after we're done."

"Understood."

Vladimir glassed the trawler a couple of miles away. Hu stopped at his net. The lights illuminated the trawler's deck and the surrounding water. The picture behind the trawler was eerie, dark grey puffy clouds formed an ugly picture. A strong wind and four-foot swells tossed Jang's boat around like a toy. The noise muted Jang's motor as Vladimir idled forward. The sea wanted him to go in another direction.

Looking through the binoculars, Vladimir observed two small outboard aluminum boats were transferred into the water with precision, they were used to help haul in the nets. All of which were full of sharks, hammerhead, and a few other large fish.

While the men in the boats were busy. Vladimir dropped anchor two hundred yards from the trawler, inflated the lifeboat, tossed it overboard, and tied it off. He needed one more thing, his AK. It hung on the hook behind the captain's chair. No magazine was loaded. He searched everywhere for it. Vladimir rubbed the back of his neck. His chest tightened. He realized Yuri never loaded it. He searched the wheelhouse for any weapon. He found a dull six-inch filet knife. *It would have to do.*

Vladimir spied the trawler; all the action was at the stern. He rowed to the bow of the trawler where the anchor line entered the water and tied off. Hand over hand, legs curled around the rope, he strained up the anchor line toward the deck. The ship's stern dropped with each passing swell; his legs flailed side to side. At the bottom of the swell before the next one hit, he found his grip and pulled himself to the top and onto the deck. He lay flat, trying to catch his breath. He peeked over a storage container and saw his target in the helm.

Crawling on the slick deck, he reached the door leading to the room below the helm where Hu was barking out orders over the loudspeaker. Vladimir figured two crewmen would be below deck getting ready to cut up and freeze the shark, while the rest hauled in the net.

With all the noise, Vladimir made his move. He opened the door next to the helm, leading down the stairs to the sleeping quarters where he had stashed a pry bar. The lock on the cabinet popped off with little effort, but no guns were to be had, just a twenty-inch machete and papers, but most important, his SAT phone and money was there. Hu continue to yell out orders topside. Three steps led up to the helm, each one creaked as he ascended, Vladimir stopped at the door. The brass knob squeaked with each millimeter of a turn. He peeked in, Hu was looking out the window at his crew on deck.

Vladimir rushed into the helm, just feet from Hu before he was spotted. Hu's head jerked back and his eyes bulged, looking as if they would fall off his face.

"What the hell?" Hu froze. Vladimir lunged at him, as Hu reached for the drawer, before the drawer opened, Vladimir stuck the filet knife into his throat. With the machete in his left hand, Vladimir sliced Hu's neck. Hu's legs buckled, blood squirted from his neck, as he struggled to remain standing. The helm splattered in red, blood dripped off the steering wheel and puddled below the captain's chair.

"It's over for you, Hu. Thanks for the sharks and your beautiful trawler; I will take good care of it. Never should you have shanked me. Now go to hell."

Hu did not last long; he bled out in seconds.

Vladimir opened the drawer next to the captain's seat and found Hu's handgun, a 9mm with a fully loaded clip. He put on Hu's old floppy hat and jacket and waited. Vladimir wanted every shark and man on board before he finished this party.

He wasn't worried about the men below deck; they would be too busy butchering the shark to go topside. Vladimir turned off all lighting in the helm. He kept the exterior lights on and monitored the crew, waiting until the small boats were stowed away and all the men were on board and waited in silence for his prey. He guessed the four men on deck had weapons; with poaching being their trade, they had to be ready.

He didn't have to wait long; a crewman started toward the helm. He back stepped to the door on the left leading to the stairs and captain's quarters and waited. A short-bearded crewman pushed through the door leading down to the deck.

"Captain, all is secure, what's next?" Before the man cleared the door, a machete found its way deep into his neck. Vladimir covered the man's mouth and set him to the deck. He never got up. Vladimir stacked the two bodies off to the side, blood flooded the helm, sloshing back and forth with each roll of the trawler, his boots soaked in the life fluid. The blood started to drain down the stairs. There was no hiding now.

Three men stood at the stern near the small aluminum boats smoking and joking around. All came to attention, throwing their cigarettes into the water, they scattered, running for their weapons.

Vladimir had in his sights what he was hoping for. The old Rust Bucket closing fast, off the starboard. He turned on all the lights, illuminating the deck and the surrounding water. Vladimir made the call. -

"Yuri, can you hear me, answer the phone,"

"Loud and clear," Yuri said.

"The men on board are all armed, pull up and look peaceful, have our men ready with the sniper rifles. Take out the three on deck, I will deal with the two below, I will wait for you to start shooting," Vladimir said.

"Understood," Yuri replied.

The Rust Bucket pulled to within twenty feet, the three-armed crewmen stood next to each other in a show of force. Yuri stepped out from the helm, waving. Before he stopped, two loud bangs. Two men dropped backward, the third started firing toward the rust bucket, windows shattering, Yuri dove for cover. The gun fire continued from both sides.

Vladimir burst through the door, two men sat on a bench seat, their legs crossed, smoking. Both men's heads jerked back, their eyes bursting from their face. Vladimir fired, two loud booms and then silence. The two men were still sitting upright, their heads forced back, pointing toward the ceiling, the cigarettes burning in their mouths, not a puff left in them.

He left the dead men behind and moved up the steps to the helm and stopped, checking for any gun fire coming from inside, there was none and he entered. Gun fire was coming from his men and return fire from one of Hu's men. He called Yuri-

"Yuri is anyone hit?"

"One man badly wounded, another cut from glass that shattered. He might not make it, we got two of them," Yuri said.

"I got the man in my sights, I need to get closer, all I have is a nine mil. The lights are going out so don't shoot anymore, I'll get him.

Vladimir turned off all the lights and under the cover of darkness, hustled down the stairs to the deck, wearing Hu's floppy hat. Vladimir made it to the small boats before Hu's man opened fire on him. He was exposed and Vladimir raised up and plunked two rounds off, wounding him. The man kept firing until a shot rang out from the Rust bucket and put him down for good.

Vladimir turned all the lights back on and waved his crew over to the Trawler. Yuri was the first one aboard after they tied off the boats.

"Yuri you're all cut up, Vladimir said.

"I'll be ok."

"Jang's boat is a couple hundred meters south. Go get it, and get back."

Vladimir pushed all the dead men overboard and returned to the helm. He sat in the captain's chair, admiring his new boat.

Yuri returned with Jang's boat in tow, both Yuri and Dmitri boarded the trawler and headed for the helm. Vladimir was sitting in his captain's chair. -

"What do you think of my new boat?" Vladimir said.

"A little bloody for my taste, but it's like new, worth a bundle, yes," Yuri said.

"Big money for the boat and shark fins in China. I have a buyer for the shark meat and the fins. Part of the crew and I will take the rust bucket back to Okhotsk and sell the shark meat and make repairs. Yuri, you, Ivan and a couple of men take the trawler and the shark fins to China.

"What about the prisoners?"

"Tie them up in Jang's boat and cut them loose."

"We be rich soon huh?" Yuri said.

"Get a couple of men over here to cut up the rest of our catch. I have a buyer for the fins, and Yuri, make sure you call me before you transfer the fins; I want all the money in my bank account first, and get someone to paint a new name on my trawler. and hopefully I'll find a buyer for the trawler too. After you make the sale, send the men to our next money-making location in America. I'll be there after I'm done in Okhotsk; call me if needed."

Chapter 15

Yuri was sixty miles east of Hainan Dao closing in on an important pay day. A patrol boat passed by going in the opposite direction. It had an enclosed cabin with telescoping radar on top, full lighting – flood and spreader – and was the size that patrolled this area, but no country-of-origin flag was flown. A cold chill went up Yuri's spine. *Who are they*? The boat slowed, as it passed his portside going south. It stopped and turned hundred eighty degrees and started to follow. Yuri increased his speed, but the boat kept pace. Yuri turned on the loudspeaker, "Trouble behind. Get ready men... Ivan, get me Vladimir on the SAT phone...

"Vladimir, we have someone following us; what should I do?" Yuri said.

"Is it the law or pirates?" Vladimir said.

"Patrol boat but no flag, don't know for sure."

"Don't panic, get the men armed and ready. If it's pirates, just take them out; if it's the law and they want to board, well we can't lose that haul, it's too much money! You have to take them down too."

"Damn Vladimir, you sure?"

"Do it, unless you want to be in a Chinese prison for life."

"You the boss."

"If it's the law, kill all and sink the boat before you leave."

* * * *

Xian turned the ship and started to follow the fishing vessel. They followed for a couple of miles, staying a safe distance. The fishing boat turned portside and increased its speed. Xian followed and pushed the throttle forward. *This guy can't outrun us, and there is nowhere to hide, what is he thinking?* Xian's throat tightened, his grip on the wheel tightened... *"God help us,"*

The patrol boat gained on the trawler, powering through the swells. Looking through the binoculars, Xian noticed a Russian name on the stern.

"This might be something men, Russian vessel," Xian said. "Be ready. If you have to shoot, make sure you hit only bad guys. Remember, Han and her uncle might be on board."

Xian called the captain of the Russian vessel on the radio but received no response. He closed to within twenty meters, close enough to use the bullhorn. "I am with AECEN; shut off your engine and prepare to be boarded."

The vessel slowed and stopped. Xian pulled alongside'- the rough sea pushed the vessels together pinching the rubber fenders flat. Xian ordered his men to tie off to the fishing vessel fore and aft.

"Prepare to be boarded!" Xian shouted.

My men are ready, all are armed, am I ready for this.? Xian was grateful for his ace in the hole, the .50 caliber mounted on the bow. Before he ordered his men to board, he heard...

"Fire, fire, fire!" Thundering booms, an explosion of

tracer rounds and bullets riddled the ship.

Xian kneeled for cover, as a trail of smoke passed by Xian's windshield, an explosion off the starboard bow, after the rocket passed over the helm into the water, the blast knocking Xian to the deck. The booms of gunfire rang loud, the windshield glass shattered flying in all directions, and a sudden coldness invaded Xian to the core. Conflicted on what to do – should he order a retreat or stay and fight. His heart raced as he watched Bo pounding away on the .50 caliber, it echoed through his ears, a unique *thump* sound you never forget. One of Xian's men lying next to him was dead. Another crewman lay out on the deck not moving.

Xian crawled over him toward the main deck. Staying below the fire, bullets exploding off the bulletproof wheelhouse above him. Bo and Cai were still alive; Bo was relentless on the .50, and Cai was firing his AK-74 toward the stern.

Xian crawled through the thick smoke onto the deck. "Stop firing, stop! Han might be on board!"

Cai seen Xian wave him off, and he stopped, but Bo heard nothing until the .50 was empty a minute later, an eerie silence forced itself onto the South China Sea. Xian's chest and stomach pained from clenching tight. The ringing in his ears was constant, he stood up to see the fishing vessel listing starboard. His patrol boat had damage but was still floating,

"Get on board, Cai, and see if Han is there before it sinks," Xian said.

Cai jumped over to the Russian vessel, AK in hand.

"All clear, no one below," Cai said.

"Thank GOD she isn't there, the .50 ripped them apart," Xian said.

"Yeah, big holes in the hull below deck might sink any second. Captain is still alive in the wheelhouse, hurt bad."

"Bo, untie the lines in case it sinks, hold on to one of them. I'll be right back; I need to talk to the captain."

Xian boarded the vessel and entered the helm. He found the captain lying on the floor, bleeding from the chest. One eye half open, blood dripped out of his ear. Xian knelt, pulled back the captain's blood-soaked jacket.

"My name is Xian, what's yours?"

"Yuri."

"Where is Vladimir? I know you're working with him, where is he? Where is the lady named Han?

"What?" Yuri whispered.

Cai came in and dropped a shark fin on Yuri's chest.

"Well Yuri, you're going to die here. You have a giant hole in your chest, and your face is in disgusting shape. You have a choice – I will push you overboard with your life vest on and let you become shark bait, or I get the information I want, and I'll get you home for a proper burial." Xian slammed a shark fin down on his chest. "I know you are working with him, where is he?"

Yuri screamed in pain, "Yes Han, we let her go, set her adrift."

"What about Vladimir, where is he?"

"Russia."

Xian removed the fin, "Where?"

That was all Xian would get, as Yuri lost consciousness.

"Xian, we need to go, it's taking on a lot of water, going to sink," Cai said.

Xian got off the vessel just as the stern submerged, leaving only the bow sticking above water line.

"That is always a weird sight, seeing a vessel sinking like that," Xian said.

"Never get used to that," Cai said, shaking his head as the vessel disappeared.

"Did you find more evidence, Bo?"

"Just a backpack with a satellite phone, money and a gun, nothing about Han and no real evidence connecting Vladimir."

"Bo, we have to bury Nobu and Lek at sea; we don't have the time to bring them home, we have to go after Han," Xian said.

Bo and Cai heads drooped; their eyes closed. They walked away as Xian pushed each man into the water. "Rest in peace Nobu, Lek. God rest your souls."

Xian and Bo shuffled back into the helm to access the damage. Xian noticed bullet holes throughout the outer shell of the hull. Looking below deck, no bullets penetrated the steel inner hull. The windshield shattered and some of the electronics destroyed but all in all the sturdy patrol boat was still operational.

"We go northeast and keep searching until we find Han," Xian said. *I don't know what I will do if she is dead. She is the only reason I took the job with AECEN.*

* * * *

Jacob was docking the sixty-foot barge, his phone

vibrated in his pocket,

"Jacob, Xian here. How's it going?

"Great, just finished hauling in the last of the plastic waste from the coast."

"Has INECE given you another assignment yet?"

"Yes, I'm going to the swamps of Louisiana. Poaching situation.

"I need your help, Han is missing."

"Missing? What do you mean missing?"

"Vladimir had kidnapped her, but we found out he let her go. She is in her uncle's boat floating somewhere in the South China Sea."

"Not going to be easy to find her."

"I was hoping you might have connections with the Philippines or Taiwanese coast guard, will they help, this is urgent. We have bad weather on the way; it is a priority."

"Yeah, we trained with both groups. I'll make a call, see if I can get help."

"Thanks, I will be heading north to search, talk soon."

Chapter 16

On the second day floating in the South China Sea, the typhoon's dark gray clouds released sheets of rain, pounding Jang's small fishing boat. The door leading to the rear deck swung open as the boat rolled portside with each swell, slamming shut, as it passed. The two doors to the storage cabinets swung open spilling more and more gear onto the floor. Han and Jang strained with each roll. The wet ropes tightened, holding them firm to the single aluminum post of the captain's chair.

Han's and Jang's hands were tied behind their backs, with their legs tied to the captain's chair. Every few seconds another swell would roll and raise the small fishing boat, opening the door again letting a river of salt water flood in.

Exhausted, soaking wet and shivering, Han struggled to loosen the ropes. The harder she struggled to free herself, the tighter the ropes got, cutting deeper into her skin. Han noticed two bolts missing from the base of the captain's chair as she pulled with her legs.

"Uncle, if you push, I think I can slide the rope under."

"Ok, I'll try." Jang's face tightened; his strength sapped; he pulled with everything he had. He was not able to raise the base high enough.

"I will pull at the same time as you push, if we time it, I might slip the rope under."

The base lifted slightly on one side, but not high

enough to slide the rope under. Then Han noticed the edge of the aluminum base. She placed her ankles over the edge and sawed back and forth, rubbing the rope against the raised edge until her legs burned. After resting to catch her breath, she started again, rocking back and forth with all her might. Han fixated on her suffering uncle, who sat in a pool of water shivering.

"Sorry I got you into this mess."

"I would do anything for you, you are like my daughter, one I never had, I'd do it again," Jang said.

Exhausted, Han rested and reflected back to better times in college with Jacob Brittles and Xian. How perfect those days were, except dealing with the JOB effect, Jacob being tested. He always made it through. I think he would say a silent prayer. *What would Jacob do now?*

* * * *

The second evening afloat, the storm continued pushing Jang's fishing boat like a rubber toy. Han woke shivering. Her fingers and hands stiff and numb, her skin raw, she went back to work. She was relentless, working to cut the waterlogged, manila rope. Wave after wave crashed over the bow, flooding the wheelhouse.

"How are you doing. Uncle?"

He moaned in exhaustion.

Han worked the rope for hours, her hope of escape faded with each exhausted stroke. They were freezing and worn out, fatigued from being jerked around by the angry sea.

"This rope seems to be made of steel; I can't loosen it. Maybe after the storm stops blowing, someone will find us; it might be our only chance."

Jang grunted.

"Are you ok, Uncle? You don't look to good; your face is pale and your hands are turning blueish."

"I can't stop shivering."

"Hang in there; the storm will break and someone will spot us, GOD willing,"

"I think we're heading northeast toward the Luzon Strait, if I am right." Jang mumbled.

"The Strait and the Babuyan Islands are the opening to the Pacific; passing that point would put us into the Pacific." Han said.

"If this storm continues for another day and we are not rescued, we might bypass the Straits or Babuyan and be living in the Pacific."

"We might never be found."

"Odds not good."

Han and Jang were exhausted. Jang was in his late seventies, maybe 110 pounds. Han sensed he was on the verge of hypothermia; his lips were turning blue; his speech was slurred. Then something caught her eye, as she wiped the tears on her shoulder. A dried fish Jang had stowed away floated under her leg. They had not eaten since the abduction, and her attention changed to food. She lay on her side hoping to snag a fish as it floated by.

The fish wasn't the only thing passing her. She had to pull up fast, as hooks and fishing gear searched for a home. The filet knife darted to and frow. It had become a game of cat and mouse, as the boat hit a swell and the fish and gear would pass by. If she timed it right, maybe. She waited for the swell to roll the boat and drain the water out of the wheelhouse. As the water drained past her, the knife did as well. Han danced with the knife and fish with each roll of the boat. She sat up.

The bow dipped, a rush of water floated the knife by Han again, and she pinched it to the floor with the palm of her hand. "I got it, Han Screamed."

Han sat up, knife in hand.

She cut the waterlogged ropes from her wrist after many short slices and then from her ankles. She crawled through the water and gear and cut Jang free.

"Hurry, start the engine," Han screamed. She stood pressing her hands against the windshield. We're about to hit the rocks!"

Jang staggered to the captain's chair and turned the ignition to start the engine. He turned the key again and again, the starter turned over but the engine would not start.

"It won't start, hold on! Hold on, rocks under bow!"

Forcefully, a sound no one on a boat wanted to hear – scraping and grinding.

Wind and waves pushed the boat deep on to the sharp crusty rocks. The bow bottomed out and stuck on the jagged rocks fifty meters from shore.

"We hit hard – do you think there is damage.?"

"I'll check it," Jang said. He opened the hatch to the engine compartment below deck. "We have a hole in the bow, were taking on water, put your life vest on."

"I think the rocks will keep us from sinking," Han said.

"If the wind and waves don't push us off, we might be

ok until the storm gone."

Han and Jang held on throughout the night, as the wind and rain continued. The moon peeked through the scattered clouds. The intense waves still dangerous but started to subside. The bow was submerged a few feet, held tight by the jagged rocks

Jang was shivering so bad, Han had to hold him up.

"The storm pushed us northeast; we must be either near the Luzon Straits or Babuyan Islands. If I'm right, we are ok Han, if we can get to shore."

Han put the semi dry fish into her pocket while Jang fiddled with the radio.

"The radio is useless, smashed up, wet," he said.

"Uncle, can you swim to shore?"

"With a life jacket, no problem."

Han eased into the water at the stern, which had started to dip below the water line.

"It's not too cold, follow me."

Jang followed. Wave after powerful wave pummeled him until he was slammed head first onto the course sandy beach.

"Dry land." Han grasped a handful of coarse sand and put it to her nose. "Salt and fishy never smelled so good," Han Screamed.

Jang dug his hands deep into the sand and flung it into the air.

"We made it, we're alive! I can't believe our luck; the pacific has to wait," Han wiped sand from Yang's face. "Uncle I'm not sure if I told you how grateful I am to have you in my life."

"I observed how hard my brother was on you."

"He never acknowledged anything good that I did. It was like I didn't exist and was never good enough, he was more involved with my brothers."

"I seen that too, that's why I took you under my wing, brought you out on my boat and taught you my fishing trade, and how to scuba dive and snorkel during the summer months, I detected something special in you."

Han bowed her head and closed her eyes, a warm feeling flooded her chest, she opened her eyes, tears pooled, "thank you for everything."

"Look what you have become, I am proud of you, even if your father isn't."

Han lowered her head, staring out to sea. "It was you who got me interested in the environment, the illegal shark fin trade and the over fishing, you are the reason for the career I have and love."

Jang watched his old boat as it slept, half sunk on the rocks. "We're alive; my boat not so lucky, it has seen its last days."

"We'll get you a new boat."

"This looks likes one of the islands near Babuyan Island," Jang said.

"Do people live here? It looks uninhabited."

"There are many of these small islands around here but I think this one might have a small village on the other side of island, I think it supports tourism."

"How can we get there? The jungle is thick with bamboo brush and wild boar and many species of spiders., I can't see any trails."

"Best way is around the jungle and over a couple hills, and hope we don't run into any snakes." Jang mumbled.

Han wiped the sand and salt water from her face. "We better rest now and start in the morning, traveling at night seems useless, you don't look good, your very pale and your hands are cold, I still see you shaking, come over here and lay down," Han drew close to Jang to provide body heat. They both fell asleep on the beach.

* * * *

Han woke to the glare of the warming sun, only a couple of lingering clouds miles to the west. *Things are finally looking good.*

"Uncle, wake up, we better get started."

Jang did not respond.

Han gently shook him. "Wake up, we have a long hike ahead."

Jang was still.

Han grasped his hand and shook. Nothing, he did not move. "Your hand is so cold," Her heart started to race, she checked for a pulse, nothing. She put her head to his chest, nothing, no beat. "No Uncle! Damn it, no!" She compressed his chest, then mouth to mouth. Back to chest compressions. She continued this until her arms were turned into heavy logs and her lungs burned. She stopped, out of breath and strength.

She pounded the sand over and over. She turned away from Jang, replaying what happened over and over again. Her chin quivered. She sat alone and stared out into the empty sea shaking her head in disbelief. Her heart raced, she wiped her sweaty palms on her shirt, Han was stuck, her mind would not free her to move. The waves crashing onto the beach grew close and forced Han to her feet. What now? Han thought. She pulled Jang away from the tide and covered her uncle in the sand and said a prayer.

Han had to leave the beach and find the village; the puny dried fish between them wasn't enough to stop her stomach from growling. She needed food and water. She hiked through the bamboo jungle and over two hills and found an easy flat trail traversing around the outer edge of the island. Two hours of hiking and a fishing village appeared.

There were a few buildings up on the hill and two sheds close to the docks where a gruff-looking old man inside was working on a net. "Do you speak English?" Han said.

"English," the sunburned Caucasian said.

"Do you have a cell phone or is there a phone I could use?"

"No phone, you have to go to the city of Aparri."

"How can I get there?"

"There is a charter, they dock down the trail at the big slip."

"When was it here last?"

The old man scratched his hairy face. "Six days ago."

"Ok, one day to wait. Thank you, sir, have a good day."

Han took the short walk to the dock, no boats. Two more Caucasian men sat fishing.

"English?" she asked.

"Yeah," the man said.

"Is there a charter boat due here today or tomorrow?"

"Not today, tomorrow."

"Is there a place I can stay the night and get something to eat and drink."

"Yeah, cottages up on the hill behind you, go to the first one, it's the manager's office, she can set you up."

Han strolled up the hill and pushed through the door of the office and rang the bell on the front desk. No one came, she rang it again and again... a stubby lady limped in from the back room. The lady's brows raised; her head shifted back.

"Hello, can I help you?"

"Yes; I need a place to stay the night."

"I don't recall seeing you come in on the charter boat last week."

"My uncle and me have been adrift for days, our boat crashed on the rocks and partially sunk, on the other side of the island,"

"Where is your uncle?"

"He didn't make it, I buried him on the beach there,"

"I am sorry, we can take you over there tomorrow and get him out of there, I will get you food and water and you can stay in the last cottage on the hill; we will get you and your uncle out of here."

"Thank you."

* * * *

The cottage was clean and the bed comfortable. One large picture window showed a beautiful view of the water. Han devoured her food and fell asleep the instant she put her head on the pillow. She woke, as the dark of the night faded.

Han left her room excited; she was on her way home. She met the hotel owner on the way to the dock. "Hello, thank you for all your help, I will be back to pay you for helping me."

"Ok, the charter should be here in two hours and I am sure they will help you with your uncle and get you to back to civilization," The owner said.

"I will wait on the dock."

"Are you sure? It's getting hot, there is no shade down there."

"I will be ok."

"Take care."

Han followed the trail down to the water. She passed by a couple of small, rundown bamboo shacks; each had shark jaws, old nets, weights and hooks hanging on the walls, an old weathered wooden bench in front, the red paint peeling. *That is a nice look for the tourists.* Past the shack she saw two Caucasian fishermen at the dock unloading full nap sacks from there fishing boat.

"What's with all these Caucasian fishermen, way out here?"

She waved to them as she got closer, one man raised up, shocked to see her standing there. One skinny man, who looked like he hadn't eaten in years, with a sun weathered face, staggered and dropped one of the bags. Shark fins spewed onto the dock. The fisherman's eyes squinted; a frown covered his sun burned face. Without a care he shoveled the fins back into the knapsack.

Han's mind exploded with heat, she ran down the dock toward the fisherman screaming, "You sons of bitches, hunting sharks for their fins is illegal!"

"Who the hell are you, lady?" A short man, no taller than Han said. Sticking his finger to her face, pushing her back. "You be wise to keep to yourself and mind your business, you understand?"

"You're not going to get away with this asshole!

The fishermen forced out a guttural laugh. "Who are you, the shark fin police. Get out of my way." He walked past her toward the shore.

The second man walked past and turned, rotating the knapsack right into Han's face, knocking her off the dock into the water. "Don't screw with me, tourist; just go about your business before you get hurt."

The men set the bags on shore and came back for the others.

Han pulled herself from the water. "Don't make things worse than they already are, boys."

"Lady! Move the hell out of my face before you get hurt!"

Han held her ground. The short man grabbed Hans's throat and tried pushing her out of his way. Han was having none of it, she took his hand and twisted his wrist backward, turned him around, and jerked him down to the ground, his wrist cracked. The skinny one came at her; he was welcomed with a swift kick to the groin and a punch to the forehead. Down he went, hitting the dock hard, face first. He lay motionless, groaning. Han reached into their boat for rope to tie them up. It was the last thing she remembered.

* * * *

"Get up you incompetent idiots, do I have to do every-thing around here?" May, the owner asked.

"We didn't think she was some kind of ninja."

"Get all the fins into the freezer, the shack is unlocked," May said

"Ok boss, what about her?"

"Check for an identification and then tie her up and take her to the shed, then clean up all that blood in your boat and on the dock. We have a charter and another of our boats coming in today. You guys better get it to-gether; we are making a lot of money here. The fishing boats and the charter business is a good cover, don't screw this up,"

"Checked out her I.D boss, says she is with AECEN."

"What, did you say AECEN?" May said.

"Yeah, AECEN."

"Shit, we have to get rid of her. You guys' finish unload-ing the shark fins and later tonight take her offshore and dump her."

* * * *

Han awoke, imprisoned. She was gagged and tied up in a weathered wooden building. Her head was pound-ing. As she examined the shed, despair flooded her mind. *I cannot believe this is happening again. At least I'm alive.* She remembered fighting with the poachers then nothing after that. She was tied to metal rods bolted to the floor and wall. The rods bolted to the floor every three feet. She pulled on the ropes with slight movement, and they burned into her already raw flesh. Han struggled to es-cape the ropes, with no luck. Anger flushed her face.

Looking through a gap in the wooden planks, the cottages were visible. Han leaned back, her head pounding. *Who hit me?*

Chapter 17

The typhoon subsided, the sea calmed, and a light wind from the south was the only lingering sign of a storm.

"Now we can cover some water, the big swells are gone, time to find Han, the weather can't stop us now. There had been no sighting of Jang's boat, A cold sweat pooled on Xian's forehead, *where in the world is she?* Xian turned off the engine and floated.

"Why have we stopped?" Bo said.

"I want to see which direction the current is going to take us; if the Russian wasn't lying, this might give us their direction," Xian said.

Xian marked his location to the land mass to the west. Ten minutes later he identified the direction he had to go.

"The current is pushing us northeast. Men we're headed for the northern end of the Philippines and Luzon Straight," Xian said.

Xian pushed the patrol boat to its limit; hour after hour, the bow rose up and descended, a constant jolt rocking the crew. The sturdy patrol boat was built for high speed and this pounding; Xian did not let up on the throttle. Between the mind-numbing pounding, an unexpected voice was heard over the ship's radio. The voice brought a sense of calm and ease to Xian. His grip on the wheel loosened.

"This is Coast Guard chopper *Flyer One*, come in,"

Jacob Brittles said.

"Yes, I hear you loud and clear. It has been a long time my friend. How were you able to get away from your work on the Oregon coast and help us out?"

"I am between assignments; there is a big poaching problem down in Louisiana. I have some time to help a friend before the plans are complete."

"Where are you now, Jacob?"

"We left the Philippines two hours ago. Your boss told me more about Han and her uncle but he gave no further information about her whereabouts."

"Yeah, we will find her, if it's the last thing I do," Xian said. "That lunatic, Vladimir needs to go down.

"Hope she's still alive!" Jacob said.

"Yeah, she is, I have to believe she is."

"What kind of boat is she in?"

"A small fishing boat, eight meters long."

"Which direction is your search?"

"We are going toward the Luzon Straits."

"That makes sense; the storm was blowing that direction."

"Yeah, current is still flowing strong in that direction."

"We will find her, Xian. I am headed for the Luzon Straits and will make sure they haven't floated into the Pacific. I will keep you informed."

"Jacob, I found out it was Vladimir who poached all those seals on the Oregon coast, my intel says he is headed for America again," Xian said.

"Where in America?"

"He did say he was going to have bears, alligator, deer

and birds for sale."

"That does limit his location. Good work Xian. *Flyer One* out."

* * * *

Two and a half hours into the air search, Jacob passed the Luzon Straits and extended twenty miles into the Pacific. There was no sign of any fishing boat. He asked the pilot to turn toward the Babuyan Islands. They started the search at the northern most island; flying around, they found no boat. There were two of the smallest islands close by, the last two before the main island of the Philippines. The coast guard BO-105 Helo circled the eastern side of the larger of the two islands.

"Do you see what I am seeing?" Jacob said to the pilot.

"Roger."

"Let's get closer."

The helo lowered, hovered over the wreckage. "That is a fishing boat, about the same size and color that Xian described," Jacob said.

"Do you see any survivors?" the pilot said.

"No, we need to search the rest of the island; I'll let Xian know what we found," Jacob said. "*Sea Warrior, Sea Warrior*, come in, this is *Flyer One*, do you copy?"

"*Flyer One*, this is *Sea Warrior*, go ahead, over," Xian said.

"*Sea Warrior*, I have spotted wreckage on the rocks at the Babuyan Islands, the smallest isle closest to the north shore of main Island of the Philippines, continuing the search inland, have seen no sign of them yet."

"I should be there in a few hours, *Sea Warrior* out,"

Xian said.

"That narrow beach over there, looks like the obvious place to set me down," Jacob said.

"Roger that."

"What is that down there? Looks like a bamboo cross, or is it just two sticks lying together? Set me down on the beach."

"No can do, not enough room, my rotors would hit the trees, too narrow."

"Get me close to the water, I'll jump."

"Roger."

"Fly over the village after you drop me, if you see Han, inform Xian," Jacob said.

"I don't have enough fuel, need to refuel in Luzon now.

"Roger that, I will hike through the jungle to the village, after you refuel come back for me."

Jacob uncovered sand and observed two boots; men sized. He covered them back up and said a prayer. The bamboo trees were thick, so thick sun rays struggled to reach the jungle floor. A few yards in, Jacob noticed fresh bamboo branches broken, his posture stiffened. *I think everything is going to be ok.* He increased his pace, dodging bamboo trees, as he shuffled deep into the lightless jungle.

Thirty minutes into the light obstructed jungle, Jacob's boots skidded to an abrupt stop, his shoulders curled forward. Water stretched out in both directions, thick bamboo and plants littered the murky water. Jacob took a deep breath. *Nothing is ever easy.* The worst of it blocked Jacob's path, the zigzag shaped webs connected to every tree and to its neighbor, each having an owner, a yellow and black devil lurking. Chills covered Jacob's entire body. Retreat was not an option. Han's safety tortured his mind. Jacob broke off a bamboo branch, his only weapon against the eight-legged devil.

Jacob creeped into the murky knee-high water. Each step in the muddy bottom devoured his boots while above him the yellow and black devils moved about their five-foot webs patrolling. Sweat soaked through his shirt, as he tore down web after web. The devils scurried for the trees or floated away in the water. *How in the world did Han make it through this nightmare?* After three hours of struggle, Jacob noticed the bamboo started to thin. Rays of sunlight gained a foothold onto the jungle floor. The jungle disappeared and opened up, Jacob wiped sweat from his forehead and entered a clearing, a small resort village next to the water appeared.

Exhausted, Jacob used his shirt and wiped sweat from his hair and face. He stumbled back, as he sat on the small hill above the village. He did not see any sign of Han. He did see a sign in front of one of the cottages, **OFFICE**, in large bold letters above the door.

* * * *

Jacob forcefully pushed through the office door.

Standing behind the desk, a short chubby woman glared Jacob down. "Hello sir, how can I help you?"

"I'm looking for my friend and coworker, an Asian woman, her name is Han. Have you seen her?"

"Yes, nice friendly girl, not sure if she is still here, I'll go check with an employee to find out, wait here."

"Do you have water I could have?"

"I'll get you one,"

"Thank you, ma'am."

"Hear you go."

May walked uphill to a secluded cottage covered in dense bamboo. "You idiots, wake up. We have a problem. The girl's coworker is here looking for her.

"What should we do?" the skinny fisherman said.

"We need to get rid of them. I'll send him to the shack where she is, take him down there and tie him up, gag him. You two depose of them far out in the Pacific later tonight."

May limped up to the office, Jacob sat on the stairs wiping mud off his boots.

"I have great news," May said. "My employee said she is resting in the shack down by the docks."

"Which shack? I noticed two of them earlier."

"The one with the nets and shark jaws hanging over the door."

Jacob shook his fist in triumph. "Thank you, thank you so much."

May started a conversation, asking meaningless questions to delay him, but Jacob was out of her office and ran for the shack. His heart was pounding as he stopped at the door, he took a deep breath and opened it.

"Han," Jacob shouted, "what the hell?"

Jacob eyes blurred, stars swirled in his head.

* * * *

Jacob woke to a muffled voice and a punching on his leg. Groggy, Jacob sat on the floor stooped over, feet and hands tied up, gagged. Han tied next to him was punching on his legs. Both of them were tied to a metal pipe screwed to a rotted wooden plank. Jacob pulled on the rope, but the pipe did not budge. He gestured to Han for help. Together they pulled with their arms and pushed with their legs. There was a cracking sound and another. They pushed in unison with all strength they had until a large split formed. Both their wrists began to shed skin form rope burns. One more pull and the pipe detached from the broken plank. They slid their hands off the pipe and worked the ropes off their hands and feet.

"I'm grateful and relieved to see you alive, Han."

Han took a deep breath. "It's been hell." Her voiced cracked. "My uncle passed away."

"I've seen the grave. So sorry Han."

"Thanks."

"Why are these lunatics doing this to us?"

"I saw the shark fins and confronted them, I think the old lady hit me from behind and they got my I.D."

"They know who you work for? Dam they are going to kill us; they have no choice."

"Not the brightest thing I've ever done." Han said.

"No, not the smartest. Let's focus on getting out of here alive," Jacob said. "How many are there?"

"Little lady May is the ring leader, and I believe there are four men, probably armed."

"Great, we're outnumbered and have no weapons. Look for a knife or anything to use Han. I will use this." Jacob ripped the pipe from the wooden plank and swung it a few times. "This will do just fine."

"No weapons, but these knapsacks in the freezer are full of fins."

"They will pay," Jacob said.

The heat of the day had long disappeared. Jacob did not see one light on in the village, peaking through a crack in the wall. He checked the door for a weakness, but remembered it was reinforced with metal stripes and a heavy-duty padlock.

"What is the plan, Jacob?" Han said.

"Get that fishing net off the wall and work quietly."

Jacob spied into the village for hours, hoping to see what might be coming. He saw nothing until the door knob to the shack turned. Han climbed onto the counter to the right of the door, and Jacob hid to the left with the three-foot-long pipe at the ready.

A tall bearded man came through the door first, and Han dropped the net over him. He struggled to escape, as the second short bald man raised his gun. He was met with a blow to the back of the head from a metal pipe. He fell face first to the ground and slept. Jacob put the pipe to the back of the head of the bearded one, as he struggled to escape the net. He stopped the short man with a blow to the stomach and one final blow to the face.

"Han, shut the door and retrieve their guns," Jacob said.

Jacob tied and gagged both men. He circled the net around both men and pounded three-inch-long steel fishing hooks into the wooden floor, pinching the net tight.

"What next?" Han said.

"Those two are going nowhere, we need to get the ring leader and any others involved," Jacob said.

"She is probably in the office."

"A lot of open ground before we reach the office…Han, stay here and guard these criminals; I'll get the ring leader and anybody else. They're not expecting me, I'll have an advantage."

Jacob left the shack into dark village. Only a faint light from inside the office gave the village life. Jacob used the palm trees for cover all the way to the steps of the office. He saw the ring leader May through the window, talking with two men. Both armed with long guns. He moved up the stairs to the door, his breathing increased as he listened.

"The others are getting rid of our trouble as we speak, you two take the boat and circle the island and see if there are others," May said. "Get rid of any and all evidence."

Jacob took a deep breath through his nose and exhaled from his mouth, his heart slowed, drops of sweat trickled down into his eye. He had to make his move. He checked the door knob, and it turned. He did not hesitate, Jacob pushed open the door, shouted, - "Drop your weapons!"

Both men raised their guns. Jacob fired, hitting both men center chest before either fired off a round. Both dropped to the floor, exposing the blood splattered back wall. May sat in her chair, wide eyed and frozen.

"Get on the ground, face down." She slid off her chair, her face smelling dirt and wood.

Jacob used a whole roll tape on May's desk and strapped her up tight.

"How does it feel, you piece of dirt?" Jacob said.

May said nothing. He checked for a pulse on the two downed men and found none.

Jacob gathered up the long guns and forced May to her feet. "Get out and start walking," Jacob said.

Han stood in the doorway of the shack, a smile on her face. "Need some help?"

"Under control. What about those two laid out on the deck of the office?" Han said.

"One is dead, the other hasn't said a word, might be dead also."

Han stared down May. "Go to hell May, your freedom is over," Han said.

Jacob pulled the 3-inch hooks pounded into the floor and lifted the man to his feet. Han tied his hands behind his back and led him outside and set him in the dirt in front of the shack next to May and secured their legs with heavy duty fishing line.

"What next, Jacob?"

"Xian should be here anytime, and my pilot is due back from refueling soon, so we wait."

Jacob and Han made their way down to the docks and sat with their feet extended into the water.

Jacob squeezed Han's shoulder. "Sorry about your uncle."

Han stared into the water, her legs swirling in the cool water... "Thanks. He became hypothermic, I don't think he weighed more than 90 pounds. I wish I never got him involved."

"You can't blame yourself; he wanted to help you."

Han shook her head, her lips tightened. "Seeing his lifeless, frail body lying there was the saddest moment of my life."

"We need to put blame where it belongs – the Russian. I will do everything in my power to take him down, all my connections will be brought to bear, we will get him if it's the last thing I do.

"He has an army; it won't be easy."

"It's me or him at this point, and with the good Lord's help, he will go down. By the way, how did you like going through the water and the spider world to get here?"

Han glared at Jacob, her lips curled up in a smile, "I came up to the water and web's and said 'No way, this is a Jacob-JOB moment, not mine.' I went right for about 200 meters and found a nice easy trail that led all the way to the village."

Jacob turned toward her, wiped sweat from his forehead, "You made a good choice."

Han laughed. "You went through it, didn't you?"

Jacob shrugged; a guttural laugh exploded from deep within. "It was a nightmare."

"Did Xian ever tell you he proposed to me,"

"No, not a word,"

Han shifted to face Jacob. "I turned him down,"

Jacob's face tightened. "Why."

Han's head lowered; her eyebrows raised. "You are the reason."

Jacob's head tilted back. "Me, why me?"

"Forget what I just said, hey look over there," Han said.

Xian's boat sped into view. He slowed seeing his friends relaxing on the dock. Pulling to the dock, his arms stretched out.

"A little late, same old Xian," Jacob yelled.

Xian tied off at the end of the dock, close to Han and Jacob.

"About time Xian," Jacob said.

"Yeah. Han you, ok?" Xian said.

Han's eyes closed. "Yes, I'm fine."

"I got here as fast as the boat and sea let us," Xian said.

Jacob pointed over to the shack. "We've taken care of the criminals here. Only two live bodies left, more in the shack and the office."

"Criminals? What criminals?" Xian said.

"Han will give you the complete report," Jacob said.

"I will get my men to take them aboard," Xian said.

"The Coast Guard pilot should be here soon; I will have him call the Philippines Coast Guard to pick up the prisoners from you," Jacob said.

"Roger that Jacob," Xian said.

Jacob placed his hand over his heart. "Well guys, it's been fun working with you two again."

"Don't make it a habit, Jacob Owen Brittles," Han said.

"I am headed for the swamps of Louisiana for my next assignment, how about you two?" Jacob said.

"Back to Vietnam for me," Han said.

"I am headed back to Hong Kong, hoping Vladimir will call for a meeting or wants to sell his product." Xian said.

Chapter 18

Jacob arrived at the dealership in Baton Rouge at 8 a.m. sharp. Carl French, a coworker at INECE met him in the parking lot. Carl was of a short stature, no taller than 5-feet-5. Gold and black framed glasses rested on his pale face. He was part of a small support staff for the field operators. He spent most of his time in the office working on paperwork related to the company's purchases.

"Hello Jacob, I've not seen you around the office much," Carl said.

"Yeah, been on a short road trip helping friends and me and Kate took a little vacation."

"The man standing in the doorway is the salesman who sold me the boat, Pete Masters is his name,"

Pete Masters had a big smile on his face, pushing open the door to the showroom. "You must be anxious to complete the paper work and get your new boat on the water, Carl."

"Yeah, this is the new captain, Jacob. He is in charge," Carl said.

Carl signed off on the endless paperwork and Pete escorted them to the doors leading to the boat yard; he paused, turned around with a big smile. "Are you ready to see your new boat?"

"I sure hope you bought a worthy boat, Carl," Jacob said.

"Best boat you can buy," Pete said.

"Let's see it," Jacob said.

They followed Pete to the 21 Swamp Shark metal boat. The boat was spotless, a powerful look. As they walked up to the flat bottom boat, Jacob hoped it performed as advertised. Jacob boarded, there was a depth and fish finder mounted on the dash. Spot lights on port and starboard, comfortable high grade vinyl bench seat, protected by a windshield.

"You did right on this one Carl."

"Much appreciated, thanks."

"You got a great deal on this boat Jacob, I made almost nothing on the sale," Pete said.

Jacob put his hand over his mouth and stared toward Pete, his eyes widened, "Ok, the boat looks good, I hope it performs like it looks."

"Top of the line, I would say the best boat you have ever been on," Pete said.

Jacob was silent as he began hooking up the trailer. Pete continued trying to convince them how little money he made on the sale and how great the boat was.

"Hey Pete, you do realize the sale is complete?" Jacob said. "Carl, time to go, get in the truck."

Jacob pulled out of the lot, boat in tow. He shook his head. "Did Pete seem a little shady to you, Carl?"

"Most salesman give off that vibe."

They drove a short distance to the dirt road leading to the public launch in the Atchafalaya National Wildlife Refuge near Bayou Manual Road. No one was at the old rundown boat launch. They stopped the truck close to the ramp.

"Carl, get all the gear in the boat, don't forget the twelve gauge and my fishing gear, I plan on dropping in the line after our inspection of the boat," Jacob said. He removed all the tie downs and put the drain plug in. "Carl, you think you can back the trailer in the water?"

"Never done it, I will try."

Jacob boarded the 21 Swamp Shark, and Carl began to back the trailer. Jacob threw his hands in the air as Carl struggled backing the trailer. Left, right, left, back and forth the trailer went. Carl had it jacked knifed after a few tries. Jacob let out a thundering laugh.

"Straighten it out and try again Carl," Jacob yelled.

Two more attempts, and Carl had it in the water. The engine started right up, and Jacob backed the boat off the trailer. Carl pulled the trailer out of the water and parked the truck and trailer not far from the launch. It was not the perfect launch, but it did float off the trailer without an issue. Perfect launches were not always the case early in Jacob's boating life either. Jacob picked up Carl on the rotting wooden dock. They started the shakedown of the Swamp Shark mid-morning, and it was performing better than Jacob had hoped for.

Jacob's adrenalin increased, as he hit the throttle. He was excited driving a new boat in a new location. The Atchafalaya National Wildlife Refuge was supposed to have an abundant and diverse wild life; there is black bear and crocodiles at the top of the food chain and deer, birds, snakes and many species of fish. There were many migratory birds so hunting them is a big deal here at certain times of years.

The sun was in full display, temp in the 80s, and humid. Jacob's assignment was simple, find and arrest poachers. The report was massive animal poaching and sale of local animal life, decimating the indigenous population.

Jacob started out slow on the water getting a feel for the boat and the surroundings of the swamp. He increased the speed once he became familiar with the boat and swamp. They started in a northward direction until coming to a channel split.

"You always go right," Jacob said.

They went right. The channel was forty feet wide. Buttonbush and Willows dominated the banks with Cypress and tupelo trees. Spanish moss hung from each. They traveled up the channel for twenty minutes and then another decision, three channels to choose from. They motored up the center channel for another thirty minutes, they slowed entering a wide body of water, lake size. Jacob had the depth finder on and it read an average depth of 7 feet. He pushed the throttle and sped across the lake. They stopped in a small cove on the far side.

"This boat is even better than I originally suspected Carl, good job," Jacob said.

"Yeah, it flies across the water."

"The Swamp Shark planes out as fast as any boat I've been on, perfect for the swamp."

"Did you see those three boats going up that channel over there," Carl said.

"Yeah, I will follow up on that route later this week; today we test drive and fish," Jacob said. "This spot looks as good as any, time to fish."

"I'll watch, thank you."

The fish finder was showing a few fish, not as many as Jacob hoped for but he started fishing there anyway. He caught a small catfish right away and tossed it back.

"Carl, do you have any updates on the worldwide food shortages?" Jacob said.

"There is no good news, people are becoming more desperate and were paying outrageous prices for food, only the rich people in poor countries can afford to buy the meat now, the poor are starving or eating whatever they can scrounge," Carl said.

"Kate and I helped Senator Norin of Oregon on his campaign, well just a couple of days for me, she believes he is a great man and environmentalist and will help solve the shortages. I'm not so sure. His speeches stress environmental concerns, but he is a politician," Jacob said.

"I understand people are becoming rich selling meat of all kinds to countries in Asia and Russia, the food shortages have hit the hardest there, the many years of draught and numerous national disasters have taken its toll."

"I have heard the same, how did you get involved in campaigning for this senator?"

"Because of Kate! what do you say we move to another spot, not much action here," Jacob said.

"You're the captain."

Carl pulled the anchor, and they headed out of the cove toward another channel. Jacob turned onto the same channel Carl seen the three boats go up, thinking they might be heading to where the fish are. Thirty minutes up the channel they came to another split. They took the channel on the right; it was narrow but deep. They traveled on this channel to another wide opening; this opening was small but the depth/fish finder did show a lot of fish. The water level was lower compared to the last stop. They dropped anchor on the far side and started fishing.

Carl leaned back in the boat. Sweat formed on his forehead under his cap. "I have seen a few alligators on our way over here!"

"They better stay away from the fish I am going to catch, the food supply must be good for them here," Jacob said.

"Better the fish, than me," Carl said

No sooner than Carl dropped anchor Jacob had one on the line, a big pull, the rod bent over, close to the water. It was putting up a good fight, but after a couple of minutes, he had it out of the water. Jacob raised the tip high to pull the fish out of the water, Carl had the net ready, he dipped the net into the water ready to land the fish. They spotted a large wave rushed toward them. Out from under the green wave, a mouth full of teeth emerged from the dark murky water and snagged the fish off his line.

Jacob's heart pounded. "Wow! That was awesome."

Carl picked himself off the deck, breathing heavy. "That was a close call."

"Did you see the size of that monster's head?" Jacob said.

"Yes, I did, how much longer are we going to be out here? I have some paperwork to complete."

Jacob held his arms up in the air. "That was cool, how about lunch?"

"Lunch at the local café?" Carl said.

"No. Over there we'll have lunch."

Carl pulled anchor and Jacob drove to a small patch of dry land nearby and beached the Swamp Shark. Jacob tied the Swamp Shark off to a cypress.

"Carl, I'm going to take a walk before lunch, I want to scout the channel where the three boats cruised up, if it looks promising for fishing, we will explore up there after lunch."

"I will stay in the boat," Carl said.

Jacob stretched his arms out wide and smiled. "Keep the shotgun handy; that gator might like you for a snack."

Jacob made his way through thick vegetation toward the channel. The trees and foliage dominated the landscape, but no trail was found. The bald cypress trees were the most spectacular and ominous looking, especially with the Spanish moss hanging from its branches. Jacob was out of his element and the unknown lurked around every tree, every bush, the monsters in the murky water below concerned him the most.

He spotted the water through the thick vegetation, forty feet away. Voices down by the water grabbed his attention. He pressed forward, toward a large cypress. Two men armed with hand guns appeared, looking like they were guarding something. Jacob's body tensed; he froze and hid behind the cypress.

Jacob's instinct took over; he moved closer and recognized they were not fisherman setting up camp. *Lord, don't let this be a JOB moment.* Jacob crawled closer. He recognized the foreign accent; Russian... Poachers.

He dropped to his stomach and crawled closer, He saw three men working the camp. His face heated, the reason he was here was before him. There were alligator, bear and deer skins hanging out to dry on ropes, tied between the trees. They had beavers, muskrats, deer and more. Ducks were plucked and being put into bags and stored in shipping containers, large containers.

A sudden chill hit Jacob's core. The size of the operation shocked him. *This is pure evil; they must have hundreds of alligators and hogs.* One man was stuffing bags filled with meat and loading it into the container. The other two processed the meat like trained butchers.

Jacob crawled to a container; inside freezing cold air punched him in the face. Two generators purred as they powered the containers and the camp.

These were well-organized poachers; all were strapped with automatic weapons. Jacob was outnumbered and outgunned; he had no choice; retreat was in order for now. He crawled away from the containers toward Carl. He had to get out and get local law involved.

Jacob crawled toward safety. A hundred feet from the camp near the water he saw Carl standing there waving at him. Jacob put his finger to his mouth and signaled for Carl to get down. Carl raised his arms to his side, shook his head and dropped to his stomach behind thick vegetation. Jacob eased his way toward Carl.

"What is going on?" Carl said.

"We have stumbled on a poacher's camp. Let's get back to the boat. Take it slow and be quiet."

"Yeah, time to get the hell out of this," Carl said.

"The boat down there was one of the same ones I saw going up the channel earlier in the day. We are aware of six of them and maybe more, we have two choices; we can go down there take these three by surprise, take their guns, and wait for the rest of them, but if the remaining four come back while we are fighting, it will get ugly.

"Yeah, we need to get out of here now and call for backup," Carl said.

"I think we can take them; we have surprise on our side."

"You are out of your mind."

"The problem is we only have one shotgun, and they have automatic weapons. If it went bad, we would become gator bait, no better way to go, then by being gator bait"

"You are crazy! the risk is just too high, I work in an office," Carl said.

"I think these guys are involved in this world-wide smuggling operation and selling it to the highest bidder in Asia or Russia. This is the exact reason I was assigned here, to stop this kind of criminal activity."

They started crawling their way to the 21-swamp boat and Jacob realized he hadn't taken a picture of their operation with his cell phone. He had to have proof to show the local authorities and the INECE for prosecution. He crawled back to the water, took five pictures, and crawled back, looking over his shoulder to see if they had seen or heard him.

Carl was a short distance away signaling for Jacob to stop. Jacob noticed two men had stopped moving things into the container and started talking. Jacob froze, and his heart thumped into his wet shirt. He kept his eyes on Carl, who had a good view of the camp. Carl waved Jacob over and they hustled back to the boat.

"Did you get the pictures?" Carl said.

"Got em, I'll send them off once we get back to the boat.,"

"No signal out here; I saw them talking on a SAT phone though," Carl said.

"Did they look agitated?"

"They did not seem to be. We better go now!"

Chapter 19

Jacob backed the boat off the shore and idled the Swamp Shark toward the dock and out of the swamp. Half way across the lake, the propeller hit something, he stopped and steered in another direction and again the propeller hit something.

"What is going on, my prop keeps hitting something," Jacob said.

"Go that way," Carl said.

"See the water behind us? We're stirring up mud; the prop is hitting mud on the bottom. We have a problem, Carl."

"What now Jacob?"

"The water level seems lower than earlier today."

Jacob raised the propeller as high as possible without it breaching the water completely. He pulled the throttle back, the prop struggled to turn, he pulled the throttle all the way back, the prop began to spit up mud and water. The 21 Swamp Shark loosened off the bottom, Jacob pushed the throttle forward and sped across the lake. They made it to the other side and were about to enter the channel, their boat abruptly stopped. Carl landed in the front of the boat, and Jacob's chest deflated into the steering wheel. He struggled for air. His chest throbbed.

Gasping for air, Jacob called out, "You ok Carl?"

"If we make it out of here, maybe."

Jacob Brittles eased the throttle into reverse, hoping

to back out. The boat didn't budge. he took it out of reverse and moved the throttle forward, the bow lowered as he inched the throttle forward. and still no movement. He attempted this a few times with no movement forward or backward.

Jacob shook his head, pounded on the steering wheel. "We are stuck, Carl."

"What have you gotten us into, Jacob?"

"We have two choices, as I see it, Carl. We can wait around until the water level rises again or..."

"Or what?"

"A trick my father taught me. We can throw the anchor out and hope it sticks to the mud on the bottom and we pull our way out."

"I would rather try and get out of here than just wait here for the water to rise," Carl said.

"There is some dry land on our starboard, I am not sure how dry it is, but if I can get over there with the rope, I will try and pull us out while you use the rope and anchor to pull from inside the boat, we might find deeper water ahead."

"That sounds like it might just work, better than sitting here," Carl said.

"Keep an eye out for alligators Carl!"

"Thanks for the reminder. If we get out of here, remind me to never work with you again."

Jacob tied the rope around his waist, grabbed the shotgun and eased his way into the water.

"Jacob Brittles, you are crazy."

Jacob waded through the brackish water and made it

to the dry bank safely. He wrapped the rope around a tree for leverage and started pulling, while Carl worked the anchor. The boat began to move, inch after inch. Jacob moved to the next closest tree and they moved the boat three more feet. Sweat rolled down Jacob's face as he pulled the boat to within five feet of the opening to the channel and deeper water.

"Were going to make it Carl, freedom ahead," Jacob said.

Carl raised one hand into the air in victory, just as two booms shook the quiet swamp, bullets began punching into the 21 Swamp Shark.

"The poachers!" Carl yelled.

"Keep using the anchor to pull you out; I will keep them busy with the shotgun; you should be able to use the anchor to pull the boat into the channel, it should get deeper not too far from here. Once you are in the channel don't stop for me, use my cell phone to call for help once you get a signal."

Jacob crawled from cypress tree to tree, and when in range he opened fire. Both poachers dropped for cover. Jacob wasn't sure if he killed, wounded or missed them. There was no movement in the boat. Carl was nowhere to be seen. *Thank God, he made it.*

Jacob moved closer and fired another round into the boat, blowing a hole in the side of the aluminum hull. The poachers shot wildly, tree's exploded, branches dropped, leaves littered the sky. The two-cypress knee protected Jacob from death. They fired their automatic weapons and stopped only to reload, before they did, Jacob stood up and fired two slug rounds, hitting both men, one in the chest and one in the head. He loaded another round in to the chamber and kept his aim on the boat and waited for any movement.

Jacob rolled on to his back, sinking into the mud, his heart stopped trying to escape. He contemplated his next move, If Carl made it into the channel, it would still be hours before help arrived. How far he got was just a guess. Jacob hoped Carl had paid attention on how to operate the boat and the directions to get out.

Jacob first priority, confiscate the poachers boat. Night was on its way, and he did not want to be squatting on this patch of dirt. The possibility of a monster alligator or poisonous snakes crawling up on him gave him chills., and the boat would be much safer, if it wasn't going to sink.

Jacob waded into the water, not wanting to make any splashing noises. He swam over to the boat and crawled in from the stern. Blood was splattered everywhere; the two men were lying face down on the deck.

Jacob's head dropped; his mouth dry. He stood over the death he was force to unload on these criminals, a miserable sight, but they gave him no choice; it was them or him. Looking at the men as they were, lying in a pool of blood and water. *Crime does not always pay.* Jacob thought.

Jacob did not want to throw them overboard to be eaten by the alligators. He started up the engine and drove to dry land and planted the bow on the bank. Next, he pulled both men off the boat, searched them for identification, but found none. He buried them in shallow graves, said a quick prayer, and motored away toward the poacher's camp.

Jacob drove back toward where he and Carl had lunch. The area was somewhat secluded. He reached the area and beached the boat just as night fell. He threw down a couple of life vests and laid down to rest, he closed his eyes and fell asleep.

He awoke to the boat being tossed from side to side. Jacob rose up to find the boat surrounded by alligators trying to get into the boat. They were giants, fourteen to fifteen feet long some of them. It would not be long before they sunk the boat if they kept trying to get in. The smell of blood in the boat had to be attracting them. Jacob did not want to use the shotgun or the newfound AK-74's, it would attract unwanted attention. He had no choice; he had to abandon the boat and take what he needed with him.

Jacob didn't want to stay near the boat; he had to find some kind of shelter for the night. The poachers camp came to mind, on top of the container would work; he would hide there undetected and off the ground, protected from the elements, snakes and alligators. It would be worth the risk. He headed for the poacher's camp hoping no one was there. He wasn't sure how long he slept, but it was late.

This has to be the darkest place on the planet, Jacob thought.

Jacob was about halfway to the camp and hide one AK-74 and the rest of his gear, he wanted to go in as light as possible. He went with one fully loaded AK and two rounds in the shotgun. Jacob was within sight of the camp; only one light was on. The light was coming from one of the containers. Jacob walked around to the back side of the container, at the opening he stopped and peeked in – there was a man standing there with knife cutting up some meat, they locked eyes, The poacher froze for a split second; his next move cost him his life, he threw the knife at Jacob and then reached for his gun on the table across from where he was standing. Jacob had no choice; he fired a shot from the shotgun and blew the man off his feet. The man moaned for a few seconds and left this world.

Jacob's heart raced and escape flooded his mind. Men scrambled in the camp, yelling in a language he did not understand. One thing he did understand was the gunfire directed at him, as he ran back into the woods.

Jacob weaved his way through a maze of trees and brush. The boat was surrounded by monstrous gators trying to get into it. He leaped into the bow and started up the engine. He put it into reverse, bullets whistled past, hitting only the darkness of the swamp. He returned fire with the AK-74 as he put the boat into gear and sped away. The gunfire stopped long enough for Jacob to turn the only direction that was out of sight of the poachers, up the channel – the same channel the poachers set up camp. Jacob's bloodless white knuckles buried the throttle as he rushed past the camp, out of gunshot range. He expected pursuit. He had just killed one of their men and by now figured out that the boat he was in is one of theirs and the two missing men were probably dead.

Jacob's neck stiffened and his forearms tightened, as he franticly searched for a place to hide. He found over-hanging tree branches near shore and he pulled the boat toward them; the large branches hid a narrow waterway, six-feet wide, but wide enough for his boat to squeeze through. He used the paddle to test the depth. The paddle did not touch bottom. Jacob turned off the engine and waited.

Jacob searched the boat and found two full clips for the AK-74, miscellaneous boating gear, and a flare gun, which he put into his pocket. The large branches pro-vided good cover; the poachers would have to drive right up to the branches and move some smaller branches out of the way to see him. Jacob took a few deep breaths, his heartbeat slowed as he watched. Jacob heard a unique sound passing under the branches. Chills surrounded his flesh. He wiped the webs from his face and body. He searched his body and seen nothing. He sat down and scanned the swamp. A light tickle ran down his arm. he jumped out of his seat, falling to the railing of the boat. Jacob covered in chills, yanked off his shirt and through it to the floor, he peered under the shirt to see a two-inch-long spider. One stomp, flattened his mortal enemy.

Jacob flopped back into the captain's chair, he had no pain or irritation. He recognized the Golden Banana spider from his studies in college and the research of the wildlife in the swamp. He recalled that the Golden Banana spider was not too poisonous and the bite was less harmful than a bee sting.

Chapter 20

The swamp was dark as hell. An eerie silence won the night, except for an occasional bullfrog sounding off. Jacob's chin rose as beams of light invaded both sides the channel. His AK was locked and loaded. He was ready for a fight. The beams of light fought to penetrate the thick foliage. Narrow beams defeated the foliage around Jacob cutting through the branches and leaves into his hideout. Three boats idled up the channel and passed him. Jacob released the tension on his AK, and exhaled once they passed and took a deep breath.

He paddled up the narrow waterway to see where it led, praying for a way out to safety. The channel was plenty deep.

He didn't get far, the thwapping of the helicopter blades stopped him. Jacob hoped it was Carl and he found help. The helicopter was close and getting louder. It passed directly over Jacob but it was not what he was hoping for. The large transport helicopter was hauling a forty-foot container below it. Jacob realized it was not Carl but instead the poachers bringing in another container.

Twenty minutes later, the helicopter flew back over carrying out a different container. Jacob leaned forward and continued up the waterway until he was far enough out of range of the poachers to start the engine. Long stringy moss hung low over the waterway, creating a tunnel effect. Jacob pushed the throttle forward; he wanted to put some distance between himself and the poachers. He headed west, looking for a main channel heading in the direction of the boat launch.

Jacob's muscles slacked, as he made his escape. Adrenaline subsided as he cruised along, confident he had escaped. His confidence came to an abrupt stop. Jacob held tight on to the wheel. He did not see the barrier until it was too late. The barrier came out of nowhere. Jacob swerved and pulled back on the throttle, but not in time. The boat slid out of the water and up the bank on to a dry patch of dirt, sandwiched between two cypress trees.

Jacob sat up off the floor and stared at two shotgun barrels. He had no time to get to his AK. Poachers caught him. Jacob thought.

"Keep your hands where I can see them poacher," he said.

"I am not with the poachers; I am fighting against them. I just killed three of them and they are searching for me as we speak," Jacob said.

"Can you prove it? Those poachers have boats just like the one you're driving; I have been watching them since they got here."

"Check my wallet, my identification shows I am with INECE compliance and enforcement. It my job to catch these people."

"Then why are you in one of their boats?"

"The poachers attacked me and my coworker; he took off for help; and I was able to kill three of them before the rest of them took after me."

"That is quite a story. I doubt anyone could make up a story that fast."

"Can you help me?" Jacob said.

"Yes, be happy to; those poachers are brutal people. Russians I believe."

"My name is Jacob Brittles. What is yours?"

"It's Bill, but my friends call me Scat."

"Why do they call you Scat?" Jacob said.

"I can tell you the scat of every animal in this swamp. I have lived and hunted here a long time."

"You must be godsent," Jacob said.

"Not sure about that, but I will help you Jacob Brittles, let's start by getting your boat off that patch of dirt and get to my house just up the canal."

The boat slid off the muddy patch of dirt into the water. Scat raised the netting and they drove up the canal.

"Why did you have that net up, Scat?" Jacob asked.

"Those poachers have been stealing from my legitimate traps for a week now; I wanted to show them I meant business and if they continue stealing from me, there are consequences."

Jacob jabbed his finger back toward the poachers. "I need to stop these criminals now! They sought to kill me and my coworker and will kill anyone else who gets in their way. I could use your help, Scat."

"These guys are heavily armed, they act like military," Scat said. "You think you can take them down?"

"Help is on the way, and I have some military experience myself. I'm not worried about their military experience. With your knowledge of the swamp, we are at an advantage."

"Whatever you need, Jacob."

Scat's house was more like a grass shack, except for the hidden steel door in the back. The only entrance Jacob noticed. The door opened up to a large room hidden from outside. Jacob walked into the large room and to his left he noticed a hallway that was 20-feet long. Jacob was amazed by what he was seeing in Scat's house, from the outside it looks like a rundown shack but inside it is a well-built home, fort like.

"Amazing place, Scat. Are you one of those survivalists?"

"I guess; it was a passion of mine to build it like it is. The house is well protected from animals, hurricanes or humans!"

"What is down that hallway?"

"The door at the end of the hallway leads to another room that is built into that small hill on the back side of the house."

"Do you have any communications here?"

Scat shook his head. "None, the closest phone is about fifteen miles east of here, but you have to get past the poachers camp to get there."

Jacob scratched his head. "Or we get back to the boat launch."

"Still have to pass by the camp and I've seen them spying the boat launch every day."

"Help should be here by morning, but before they arrive, I need to know their number. I will recon their operation and numbers before sun up," Jacob said. He raised his chin high. "Maybe I can take down a couple more before help arrives."

"Anything I can do to help, I'm with you. These poachers have been taking food and' money from me... I legitimately hunt gators for a living!

Chapter 21

Scat and Jacob took turns guarding the entrance to the narrow waterway until the water level dropped to a depth no boat could pass.

"How long have these poachers been here?" Jacob said.

"I noticed them three weeks ago, probably here longer," Scat said.

"Have you or anybody called on the law?"

"I have no phone, and being so deep into the swamp, I doubt anybody realizes they're here."

"Have you tried to get to a phone?"

"They have the only way out of here guarded day and night and I don't want to leave my place unprotected."

Jacob rubbed his forehead. "Can we get close to the camp without going on the main channel?"

"After the water level rises, we can take my canoe around to the backside of the camp, but no guarantees we make it, depends on the water level. These guys are everywhere. They might spot us."

"After we camouflage the boat, we can try," Jacob said.

Jacob and Scat paddled southeast; the water was less than two feet deep. Cypress stumps and logs impeded every inch of travel. Alligator weed wrapped around their paddles with every stroke.

"Scat, the coast of Oregon is one of the most beautiful places on earth, but this place is its equal, but in a different way" Jacob said.

"I hope it remains that way."

The brackish water hid a minefield of underwater obstacles; cypress stumps were everywhere. Built-up silt and mud forced them out of the canoe into the water. Jacob's boots sunk into the mud and the humidity drained Jacob's energy. The swamp gas smell burned with every breath. Sweat dripped down his face into his mouth, as they pulled the canoe through the water.

"I take back what I said about the beauty of this place," Jacob said.

"Not much farther to deeper water," Scat said.

"How many things are in this place that can kill me?"

"Too many to talk about now, keep an eye out for gators and snakes."

"Don't forget the scum I'm after."

Scat and Jacob found deep water 200 feet from the camp. They paddled to within fifty feet of the poacher's camp, hidden by thick vegetation. Jacob peeked through the Spanish moss.

"I count 10 men and the one on top of the container attaching straps," Jacob said.

"I believe there are close to twenty; the others must be out poaching."

"That dude on top of the container seems to be barking out all the orders, he must be in charge," Jacob said.

"We don't stand a chance; they are all armed with automatic weapons."

"We have surprise on my side. They need to be checked and understand someone is on to them, I need to slow this massacre down, or there won't be any wildlife left."

"What is your plan?"

"I can't get you involved. What I'm about to do is too risky. Take the canoe back to your house and hunker down."

"How are you going to get back?"

"See that green boat with the windshield? That's my boat. They must have caught Carl, my coworker; I need to find out if he is ok."

"You will never make it back, if you go over there," Scat said

"I will wait till dark."

* * * *

Jacob crawled over the mud, to the edge of the water. The swamp was eerily quiet and dark, not a chirp from a bullfrog or a cricket. His temples pounded as he entered the water. Halfway across the channel, Jacob seen the faint lights of the camp through the thick brush. He swam toward the Swamp Shark. There was no one guarding the boats. He glanced over the stern. The key was in the ignition. He swam around the other boats, checked for keys, only two boats had keys in the ignition, he tossed them into the water. He swam farther down the channel to a safe distance from the camp.

Jacob crawled out of the water and crept toward the hidden AK -74. He let out a deep breath, the AK was still there. The voices of the poachers went from mumbles to coherent voice as he scrambled toward them, with his AK draped over his shoulder.

The camp was brightened with amber lights. Men worked at fast pace butchering and loading their catch. Jacob moved stealthily to the containers, there was no

sign of Carl. He scanned the camp and sighted four cam-
ouflaged tents thirty feet away. Jacob stopped at the first
tent and peeked in. No Carl, but there was one cot and
something weird stood out to Jacob – an easel with a
painting of a woman and a baby in her arms, they were
laying in snow near a broken-down bench, with a red-
tinted fog surrounding them. Jacob peered in the other
tents and did not see any sign of Carl. Another large green
canvas tent 20 feet into the deep brush was Jacob's last
hope. He approached from the backside, men were talking.

"He heard talk about their total catch and then...You
buried the man where he will never be found," a deep-
throated voice said.

"Yes, he is fifty feet back of camp, six feet deep,
Vladimir."

A sudden coldness hit Jacob's core. *Vladimir, your day
will come."*

Jacob backed away from the tent. A voice in the dark
spoke. "Hold it right there, don't move."

Jacob wielded the AK toward the voice and fired
numerous rounds at him. The man stumbled away and
fell into the mud. Jacob kept firing at the entire camp as
he ran for the Swamp Shark. Gunfire erupted; the dark
swamp turned into a light show. Jacob dove into the
Swamp Shark, turned the key and sped away up the
channel. Bullets riddled the metal hull, sparks danced
passed his head. Looking back, he seen them boarding
their boats. He pushed the throttle forward. The bow
rose into the air and planed out as he buried the throttle

forward and sped into the darkness of the swamp.

For the first time in Jacob's life, he was the chased. Three boats followed him at high speed. The Swamp Shark was a superior swamp boat and kept him out of range of their gunfire. He sped past the narrow waterway leading to Scat's place, going deeper into the swamp. Searchlights began to fade as Jacob pulled away from the poachers.

Jacob moved past a couple of narrow channels. He slowed the Swamp Shark, on the starboard a field of duckweed. Beyond the duckweed, five-foot-tall reeds. He aggressively turned into the field, pushing away the duckweed as he passed through and leaving an open water trail behind. Jacob idled through the duckweed, his depth finder sounding; it read three feet. A few feet farther in, it sounded again, reading two feet. Jacob turn- ed off the alarm; not wanting it to give him away if the poachers happened to stop their engines nearby. The duckweed reshaped the opening behind him.

Jacob idled into the tall reeds for cover. He turned off the engine and waited. Minutes later, a motor boat pass- ed by. Jacob took a deep breath.

I think I lost them. Jacob thought.

Jacob started up the engine and pushed the Swamp Shark into the tall reeds. He entered the pitch-black cy- press forest and the unknown, *what an eerie place*. He idled through the reeds with ease. His hope of escape faded. Beads of sweat formed on his forehead; adrenaline rushed through his body. Behind him, a motor idling, reeds were disappearing behind him, as voices became audible.

"He went this way," a deep foreign voice barked, as the tall reeds continued to flatten 30 feet away.

Jacob had no choice; he fired in the direction of the voices. The poachers fired back, missing Jacob and cutting down tall weeds off his starboard.

"Back out, back out!" a poacher shouted. Jacob kept firing, as he drove deeper into the thick reeds. He stopped short of exiting the cover of the reeds and listened for the poachers, he did not hear voices or a motor close. Jacob idled into the 30-foot-wide channel, surrounded by the thick cypress forest.

The entire forest was covered in Spanish moss. The moonlight struggled to reach the swamp floor. Jacob idled past a maze of cypress trees, and his movement slowed to a crawl. He wanted to get back to Scat's, but he had no idea how to get there or how to get out of the swamp. Pushing aside the moss, Jacob began to second guess why he volunteered for this assignment. He was lost in an unfamiliar world; every inch of the swamp looked the same in the dark. Spanish moss stretched down to the water, covering the channel like a cave, his visibility limited to a few feet ahead.

Losing all inhibitions, Jacob turned on his spotlight, focusing his attention to his six; there was no sign of the poachers. He approached a bend in the channel, the cypress knees disappeared, the cypress trees thinned. The propeller no longer churned up mud from the bottom, as the water level increased. His forearm muscles relaxed. The deep impressions on the steering wheel faded. A sense of calm overtook him.

The poachers must have given up. Jacob thought.

In front of him, a larger channel emerged. He used the spot light to illuminate the banks of the channel. Jacob eased the throttle forward as he entered the channel, looking in both directions. He did not see any trouble, but he did notice up and down the channel, ropes tied to trees with whole chickens attached to the end and a large metal hook hanging a foot above the water.

One by one, Jacob pulled the chickens off the hooks and tossed them into the water. He worked his way up to the last chicken, seeing through the clear water, a boat encased by water directly below the chicken. Looking closer he noticed something he wish he never seen, an image that would be imprinted on his mind for life, – the half skull of a person and a partially intact body, chained to the seat. Jacob had seen enough he had to get out of this nightmare. He drove up the channel a few hundred yards and spotted a building on the Westside, more like a shack and a boat dock. He pulled into the dock and tied off. He was hoping for help, a phone or a road out of here, something. Jacob stepped onto the twenty-foot-long newer built wooden dock.

Multiple shacks were scattered throughout the property. He advanced with caution toward them, looking in all directions. A putrid smell invaded Jacob's nose. There were numerous ponds to the left of the shacks. He searched the shacks and found no one. Some of the shacks had cots in them; others had equipment and small tanks with baby alligators in them. Jacob started to search the surrounding ponds. The putrid smell intensified the closer he got to the ponds. The smell was familiar to Jacob, rotting flesh, or something similar. Entrails and alligator's heads littered the banks outside of the fence surrounding the ponds

Jacob heard splashing at a pond hidden behind heavy vegetation. He pushed aside the vegetation. His heartbeat thrashed in his ears at the sight. Hanging from a cypress branch over the center of the pond, a man hung upside down, six feet above the water. His hands tied behind his back.

"Sir, hold on, I will get you down," Jacob yelled.

No audible words were spoken, only a faint moan. The man was stiff and hung there as if he were dead. Jacob climbed up the tree and scooted along the branch; the man hung at the end of the branch. Jacob reached the rope and began to cut, the strands started to separate. Halfway through the rope, A giant head with a mouth full of teeth leaped from the green liquid below. The mouth wide open, with water escaping, snapped shut inches from the man's head. The crunch of its teeth raised the hair on the back of Jacob's neck. Liquid droplets covered Jacob's face, as the giant gator fell back into the water. The man seemed unconscious until a strained groan was uttered as Jacob pulled him upward.

Jacob pulled with all his strength; his forearms burned; his hands turned red. *Branch don't break.* He pulled until he had the man's chest draped over the branch. He cut the rope and freed him from the torture and dragged him to the trunk of the tree, where he lowered him to the ground.

"Sir, are you ok?"

"Do I have all my body parts? I can't feel much," he mumbled.

"Yeah, you are intact, what happened to you?"

"Not totally sure yet, they killed my business partners and took our entire farm-raised alligators. I wounded one of them, but they overwhelmed me and hung me here."

"How long ago were they here?"

"I think two days."

"Are there any communications here or a road out of the swamp?"

"No phone and the water is our road."

"Did you see where the dead are?"

"Not sure, for all I know they were gator dinner."

"Let's get to my boat, I'll get you some water."

"Who are these guys? They took over my business like a well-oiled machine."

"They are part of an international poaching organization, all military trained."

Jacob helped the man into the Swamp Shark.

"We need to get out of here, those same men are hunting me as we speak, which way is out of here?" Jacob said.

The man pointed. "That way, southwest."

"That way will bring us right into the poacher's camp."

"There is one other way, but it is shallow, there is obstacles and dead wood most of the way, but it should be deep enough."

"By the way, I'm Jacob and you are?"

"Chet, if we make it through the shallows, we will end up on the backside of my cousin's place. He will help us."

"Ok, we have to try, no choice."

Jacob and Chet left the dock, as the light burned into the darkness of the swamp. The silence was mesmerizing. Tule fog floated off the surface of the water, and chills covered Jacob's body as the fog weaved over and around the cypress trees like a ghost.

They drove deeper into the swamp. Their passageway began to narrow, no wider than six feet. It was just wide enough for the Swamp Shark to fit. The water level was less than three feet.

"Chet, I need you on the bow to guide me past all the obstacles."

"I can do that."

Jacob and Chet had all their attention on what was ahead. The likelihood of escape was in front of them, Jacob's confidence grew, his wrinkled face smoothed out. Chet guided Jacob with hand signals, "Left, turn left, one foot, ok cleared." They worked together and made good progress. Until from behind-

Boom after boom erupted. Chet flopped into the water and hid under the bow while Jacob dove for cover as he fumbled for his gun. He raised his gun above the transom and fired wildly, as bullets riddled the Swamp Shark. He waited until the bullets stopped flying and peeked over the transom. The poachers were hiding behind the seats. Jacob backed up the Swamp Shark as he fired, he stopped 20 feet from the poachers, and picked up his second AK. He rested both guns on the motor and unloaded both clips in the direction of the poachers.

Once the bullets stopped flying and the swamp found peace, Jacob stood over the transom. The smoke and smell of gun powered began to dissipated. The poacher's boat was littered with two-inch holes and taking on water. Jacob backed up to the poacher's boat firing until he seen the inside. Both men were moving and moaning. "Help me please." Jacob hopped into the boat and he checked the wounds. The wounds were mortal, Jacob put life vests and towels over their wounds, nothing else he could do. He retrieved all their weapons and ammo. The poachers were shredded, massive amount of blood started to mix with the invading water and pooled around the dead.

Jacob shook his head. *I've seen enough blood to last me a life time, What a waste of life.*

Jacob idled forward. Chet glanced over a cypress knee. "Chet you, ok?"

"Once I get away from you, I might be, these guys want you bad."

"Tell me about it, my initials being what they are, it stands to reason. Jacob, you handled that with great skill and courage."

"My training took over," Jacob said.

"What training?"

"U.S. Coast Guard."

"They trained you good."

"If we keep up this pace, how long until we reach your cousin's place?"

"Around sunset."

Chapter 22

The water level began to drop, the prop struggled to turn, kicking up mud and debris and suddenly stopped turning, the Swamp Shark came to a stop.

"Chet, the hull is hitting bottom, and the propeller won't turn; we need to get out and pull the boat to deeper water, can you help?" Jacob said.

"I will give it go."

"Is it normal for the water levels to get this low? I had the same problem earlier,"

"Yes, it does get low."

They pulled from the banks of the waterway, but the deep mud, trees and shrubs made it impossible. "We need to push and pull from the water," Jacob said.

Jacob and Chet slid into the brackish water, sinking into the mud with each step. Chet pulled from the bow with a docking line and Jacob lifted the stern and pushed. The water level reached up to Jacob's knees. They pushed and pulled the boat around a maze of Cypress knees and dead wood, a foot at a time.

"Chet, have you ever seen gators in this waterway?"

"Yes, but usually small immature ones, unless a monster swims in and eats one."

Jacob put his gun on the stern, his eyes narrowed, scanning the narrow waterway. Dark clouds from the south moved over them, a scattering of water droplets began to fall. The humidity made the swamp feel like a sauna, sweat and water droplets drenched their faces. They struggled to move the Swamp Shark more than a foot at a time. The mud swallowed their shoes with every step. The light rain turned into a torrential pour. Visibility decreased as the heavy winds forced the rain sideways into their faces.

"If this keeps up and the water rises enough, we will be back in the boat soon," Jacob said.

"We will make it to the channel behind Scat's place soon if the rain continues," Chet said.

"Did you say Scat? Scat is your cousin?"

"You know him?"

"Yeah, we met, good man, hey have you noticed, it's getting easier to pull the boat," Jacob said.

"Yeah, the water level can rise fast,"

Sheets of rain pounded the swamp. The water level rose as Jacob expected, releasing the Swamp Shark from the mud and it floated free. Jacob and Chet flopped back into the boat and drove toward Scat's place.

"Thank God we're free; no gators either," Jacob said.

"Out of the water and into who knows what," Chet said.

They moved toward Scat's without obstruction, making good time. The sheets of rain settled into a light mist. Sun rays broke through the dissipating clouds. Steam rose off the water as the swamp warmed. The swamp was calm and silent until gun fire brought Jacob and Chet to their feet.

"Sounds like its coming from the direction of Scat's," Chet said.

"How much farther?" Jacob said.

"I'd say 10 minutes at this pace."

"Take the wheel, Chet; I want to make sure we are locked and loaded and the clips are full.

The closer they got to Scat's, the more it sounded like a war zone. The gunfire and grenades echoed into Jacob's soul.

"Do you smell smoke?" Jacob said.

"Yeah."

"Does Scat have any enemies in the swamp?"

"No, not anyone," Chet said.

"The poachers must have found him."

"What are we going to do?"

"We can give them some of their own medicine. Drop me off short of Scat's place, hold back in the boat, out of sight and be silent, we might need a quick escape."

Chet powered down and coasted onto the muddy bank. Jacob slid off the bow and ran toward Scat, the smell of smoke strong and thick as he approached the house. Gunfire stopped as Jacob laid down on the mound behind the house. Smoke billowed from Scat's house.

Jacob approached the front of the small house his eyes searching all directions. He found no poachers or Scat. The only sound was the popping and cracking of burning wood. The front door was gone, Jacob stared into the burning house. His stomach pained at the sight, his mouth filled with saliva, he dry heaved. A body lying on the floor was covered in flames, a shotgun barrel next to the body, half the house was enflamed the other half was smoldering. Jacob's face tightened, his jaw clenched tight, he backed away.

Jacob heard a familiar sound, as he crested the mound behind what was left of Scat's place. A chopper appeared carrying a shipping container, a man on top, holding onto one of the cables with a long gun in his other hand. Jacob and he locked eyes, the poacher waved with gun in hand and started to fire, Jacob fired back, as the chopper disappeared out of sight.

There was nothing left for Jacob to do. He dragged himself to the Swamp Shark.

Chet stood on the bow. "What's going on Jacob?"

"I'm not going to sugarcoat it. Scat is dead. They killed him, and it is an ugly sight."

Chet's head dropped; his eyes closed. "Why? He never hurt anyone!"

"These are evil people, that is why," Jacob said. "Let's get out of here; I'm sure that was the last container, they probably have cleared out by now. I'll call local law to clean this mess up after we get out of this hell."

"What's next for you Jacob?"

"Go home and wait for another shot at this killer. I won't stop until I have him, dead or alive."

Chapter 23

Vladimir landed in San Francisco for his appointment with the local Green Peace office. He checked into his hotel and made multiple calls, one to his crew to make sure they were in place and ready and to Qian, his partner in China.

Xian answered without hesitation.

"Hey partner, did your man get all the shipments?" Vladimir said.

"Yes, he did. The money will be in your account today," Xian said.

"I will have an even bigger shipment on the way once I get that money into my account," Vladimir said.

"It will be there today, where are you now? Xian said.

"That is not important, be ready for more product, we are all going to be filthy rich after this operation."

"We will be expecting your call; I am ready to be rich too."

* * * *

Vladimir arrived at the Green Peace office early morning. He was greeted by Sally Pendergrass, the Director of Finances. She handled all donations for the region. She was anxious to see Mr. Kozlov. He pledged over the phone to donate a large amount of money, $100,000 to be exact.

"I am so happy to finally meet you Mr. Kozlov, how are you?" Sally said.

"I am great and anxious to know if my request was granted for a ride along on one of your sea operations," Vladimir said.

"Yes, it was. For the donation you offered, we would love to have you aboard our ship."

"Here is the check, when do we get started?"

"We have a ship docked in San Francisco and ready for you. I can call a cab to take you to the Pier, where our ship is docked and ready to depart."

"Ok, excited to go, thank you."

"Have a great time."

Vladimir went back to his hotel and made two calls. The first was to Dmitri. Dmitri informed him they had acquired a 60-foot fishing vessel in San Francisco and were just off shore by the Farallon Islands. It was big enough for transporting all the men and equipment they would need for their next job. The second call was to a friend back home. He wanted her to call their bank in four days and cancel a check he wrote for one hundred thousand dollars to Green Peace. Vladimir postdated the check. He also had her call Pavel who was waiting on the old Russian factory ship and let them know where and when to meet him. Sally was so excited about getting such a big donation she did not even notice the date.

Vladimir mumbled, "I am a genius, I can't be stopped."

He took the cab to the Pier, and there it was. He paid the cab driver and waited a distance away from the large, green ship. He studied every movement of the crew and the general makeup of the ship. There was a rainbow painted on the bow. The helm at the front of the ship had a helicopter pad. Crew members walked the deck cleaning and checking equipment. He spied for a short while for as much information about the ship and crew before boarding.

Chapter 24

Jacob took in a deep breath of fresh cool Oregon air before opening his apartment door, overlooking the ocean. Before he could lie down, his phone pinged, Xian's number displayed.

"Jacob, I received the call from Vladimir, sounds like he is already set up for another job," Xian said.

"Do you know where?"

"No, we were able to track his cell phone call from around San Francisco."

"Do you think it's something on the West Coast again?"

"Yes, but when and where, only he knows."

"We need more information; I am positive it's the whales but where?"

"Should I go to our offices in San Francisco and try to find him."

"No, I will call my supervisor and have him line up a ship and crew for us, get up to Seattle, where we have a ship. We need to get on the water and be ready for anything," Jacob said.

"Ok, I will keep you posted," Xian said.

Jacob plopped on the sofa in his meager apartment. Kate was not home. She was still working on the senator's campaign somewhere. Jacob stretched out, closed his eyes. His mind drifted... thoughts of transferring to the swamps of Louisiana, it did not seem like a good idea now, after fighting with poachers, alligators, snakes, mosquitoes, spiders and the annoying humidity and heat.

He defeated some of his worst fears while there, which was one of the reasons he wanted to go in the first place. *Why would I leave the place I loved the most – Oregon and the ocean.* It was a tough decision, promotion more money or stay where he loved for less pay. Before any decision, Vladimir must be stopped!

Jacob and Xian reasoned Vladimir was going to poach whales somewhere in the Pacific. They also summarized the annual migration north was under way and most of the whales migrate somewhat close to the coast. Jacob was confused on how Vladimir might pull off such a brazen operation so close to shore without being seen.

Jacob hoped Xian would find more information on where Vladimir was but didn't hold out hope. If not informed, Jacob would have to find him somewhere within the whale migration path, not a great plan but it's all Jacob had to go on.

Jacob had to see Kate before he went on another assignment. She would never forgive him if he did not visit her before he left. Jacob stopped in the middle of packing for his next assignment and drove over to his parent's house to see if Kate might be there. A note on the dining room table – At fundraiser, Kate.

During his drive, he reflected about how lucky he was to have met her. Considering the way, it happened and how those circumstances brought them together. It was a typical JOB moment.

* * * *

That day started off like any other day, reading his newspaper with a cup of coffee, then a shower and off to work. Jacob took a different route that day. It was a bit longer but more scenic. Halfway there, a vibration in the rear of his car and then a loud *pop*... Dam it, a flat.

Being on a rural road, Jacob drove about a quarter mile to find a safe place to pull over and change the tire. The pullout was flat with a few weeds, a perfect spot to change a tire, someone must have known Jacob was coming. Once stopped, Jacob removed all the tools from the trunk and loosened the lugs on the rear tire. Jacob seen movement out of the corner of his eye. He took a look around but nothing was there. Jacob did not think much of it and went back to removing the tire. He removed the last lug and pulled off the tire. To his shock, two big eyes were staring at him. Jacob heart sunk to the bottom of his feet. He jumped back so fast his shoes almost didn't come with him. The snake lunged at him and struck Jacob on his pant leg. As it let go, he reached for the tire iron and was ready to crush the serpent, but it slithered past him into the brush and was gone.

Beads of sweat pooled on Jacob's forehead. He wasn't sure if he was bitten and pulled up his pant leg to check. Sure enough, a scratch and puncture, not exactly what you would think a snake bite would look like, but it hurt and bleed.

Panic started to set in. *"I have to get to the hospital fast,"* He feverishly tightened the lugs, left the flat tire, jack and tire iron on the side of the road and sped toward the hospital. He knew rattlers were the only poisonous snakes in the area, in the moment, he did not remember hearing a rattle, heat flushed his face, an uneasiness was building, panic took control, he sped even faster. Jacob hit sixty mph in turns meant for twenty-five.

Jacob's heart raced; it was twenty minutes to the hospital. Heat boiled his face, and desperation took over his mind. Jacob pressed the accelerator deeper. As his speed increased, a sign ahead stated 25 mph. Jacob hit the brake pedal hard. The wheels screamed; the car floated. He turned the steering wheel left and right trying to save the out-of-control beast. Jacob hated the beast at that moment. The beast fishtailed and confiscated the entire road. He turned the wheel back to the right and started to gain control on the turn. Around the corner, another car appeared.

The car swerved in front of Jacob and disappeared. Jacob skidded to a stop. There was a cloud of dust behind him, but no car. *God why?* This can't be happening! not another test, please. Jacob thought. His time was running out fast.

Jacob had no choice; he backed up to the cloud of dust he saw the car on its roof down the ravine about twenty feet. Jacob had to help. He grabbed his safety tool from the glove box and slid down the ravine to the car.

She was screaming, "Get me out, get me out now!"

The door was crushed and would not open.

"I am going to break the glass, close your eyes and turn your head."

Jacob put the tool to the glass, and it shattered. He reached in and cut the seat belt and pulled her from the crushed car. She started calling him every name in the book.

Jacob raised his hands, shaking his head. "Miss, I am sorry, I cannot stay and argue, I have been bitten by a snake, and I need to get to the hospital now! Are you ok to drive me there?"

"What! You're kidding. Yes, I can drive, you jerk."

"I'm sorry for causing you to crash."

Jacob explained the entire story to her, the frown frozen on her face slowly disappeared, as they parked at the hospital.

* * * *

The doctor examined Jacob's leg. "This is not a snake bite; it's more of a round cut and deep scratch not a puncture."

"Wow, all this trouble for nothing," Jacob said. "Is the girl, ok?"

"You can ask her yourself; she is waiting for you in the waiting room."

Jacob sat next to her; his lips tightened his forehead wrinkled. With a humble heart, Jacob asked "My name is Jacob, What's yours?"

"It's Kate."

"I am sorry, I will take care of everything, and I will call a tow truck so we can go get your car out of the ditch."

"Ok, it's the least for you to do," Kate said.

Every time Jacob reminisced on how he met Kate, he realized how lucky he was.

That day, Jacob wanted to surprise her at Congressmen Norin's fundraiser. He needed to spend some time with her before he went after the Russian again. Kate started working for the congressman during his last election. She believed he was a good man. Jacob never completely trusted any politician. He went to some of his speeches with Kate to see what he was all about, but Norin was just like any other politician to Jacob. Norin professed to be an environmentalist, which seized Jacob's interest. The speech sounded like lip service, but Jacob gave him the benefit of doubt for Kate's sake.

Kate was surprised to see Jacob. She had a big smile on her face. Her natural beauty made Jacob melt. She had an infectious smile. Her dark hair flowed perfectly down to her shoulders, and her hazel-colored eyes and full eyebrows floored Jacob every time he seen her. He was a blessed man.

"How are you, Kate?" Jacob said.

"Great now – why didn't you tell me you were coming here?"

"I wanted to surprise you. How is the fund raising going?"

"It has never been better. Yesterday we received the largest dollar amount we ever have, all in one day, it was unbelievable."

"Who donated it?"

"Close friends of Congressmen Norin's, there was Dave Simmons, he works in education field, also that famous TV evangelist – Ronald Milken and the other investors – I think some rich millionaires, I didn't get their names.

"Wow, this guy has some big-time investors."

"Yeah, I think he is going to do some great things," Kate said.

"With that kind of big money, he would have a big advantage in any election. What is his speech about today?"

"He is going to start with environmental issues and then finish with the economy as it relates to the worldwide food shortages."

"This should be interesting," Jacob said.

"I still cannot believe the kind of money he received from those three men," Kate said.

"It is shocking."

Jacob was unimpressed as the Congressmen talked about environmental issues; it was nothing new or different than what any other politician was saying. The topic about the worldwide food shortage came up, Jacob was curious. The congressman kept saying how he was on the verge of solving the problem. He made it sound like he and he alone would solve it. Jacob was getting bored with the man's rhetoric but sat there politely and listened until he was finished.

Jacob was shocked that the Congressmen got a standing ovation after his speech.

"People seem to like this guy," Jacob said.

"Yes, they seem to like his message," Kate said.

"Kate, I am going on assignment soon. Would you like to go to our spot on the coast for the weekend?"

"That is something I was hoping you would say."

"I have to go to the office now I will talk to you later,"

"Ok Jacob, I am holding you to that promise."

"Be ready, we're going."

* * * *

Jacob walked through the front door to his office building, hoping to get to work without interruption from his boss, who wanted a complete report before he did anything else. Jacob seen no sign of his boss so he went to work on the computer studying the migration route of whales. He recognized Vladimir had a killing pond anywhere from Mexico to Alaska. He needed more information if he was to have a chance of catching Vladimir in the act of the crime. The one sure thing Jacob understood, it was the annual whale migration north to the rich summer feeding grounds around Alaska and the Arctic Circle.

Jacob spent time talking to coworkers and people from other agencies. No one had any ideas where Vladimir's killing would start. Jacob did understand, if Vladimir got away with this cruel crime, he would make so much money, he would disappear, never to be found. The possibility angered him.

Jacob sat anxiously waiting for a call from Xian which never came. Tension tightened his throat. A sense of dread pained him. Waiting was no longer an option, he called Xian and asked if he had any news of Vladimir. Xian had no word where he might be. Both were deflated.

"This case has become personal for me and I know for you and Han as well, Vladimir has to be taken down at all costs, You and Han have been working to take him down for as long as you have been with AECEN, we have to be prepared to see it through to the end." Jacob said.

Jacob hung up and noticed his boss staring him down.

Every time Jacob's eyes rose above his monitor, his boss David Sanders was burning a hole through him with a harsh stare. He yelled out from his office.

"I need that report on what happened in Louisiana on my desk before you leave the office today, Jacob!" Sanders said.

"What is the problem boss? I always have my reports in on time," Jacob said.

"You never seem to catch anybody; you just seem to waste what little resources we have Jacob! Your inability to catch these criminals along with your associates from AECEN, we are getting further cuts to the budget."

"What are you talking about?" Jacob said.

"There is word that Congress wants to cut all funding they just started to give us."

"A complete shut down?" Jacob said.

"Yes, there are two members from Congress who are pushing hard to shut us down," Sanders said.

Jacob let the anger of his boss slide off his back like a bead of sweat. "Which members of Congress?

"One congressman is from your neck of the woods – Victor Norin – and the other is from Washington State – Anthony Mitin."

"I know of this Norin character; he is a piece of work. What do we do now boss?" Jacob said.

"Just keep working until they pull the plug."

Jacob had to get away; he called Kate to see if she might be ready for their weekend trip down the coast. Kate answered after one ring. "Kate, are you ready?"

"I need to hand in my report, I'm glad I finished it on

the plane ride home, need to get away, need a break from this place."

"When you get here, I will be ready," Kate said.

Jacob and Kate both love the Oregon Coast; it was so clean and the air so fresh. It was never crowded; most times their particular beach was deserted. They always brought a small tent and camped out on the beach, sometimes never seeing anyone the entire time they were there.

Jacob picked her up after eight. The drive down the coast was relaxing and beautiful, the blue water and clear sky helped Jacob forget about the complicated situation he was dealing with. There were no cars in the lot, not unusual for their special location. The sun had long disappeared and the moon was covered by the fog rolling in. They unpacked and set up camp and talked some about Jacob's last assignment. -

"Jacob, what happened in Louisiana?" Kate said.

"It was a disaster; most of the poachers got away."

"At least you're ok."

"We will get him, although I sometimes have my doubts."

"It sounds like these guys are relentless at what they do. You will find a way to get them!"

"We just don't have the manpower or finances they have; all our resources are tied up dealing with the worldwide food shortage. Now I hear your congressman wants to pull the plug on INECE."

"Congressman Norin, that can't be; he is running on an environment platform," Kate said.

"My bosses' words, not mine, INECE cannot spend money on this particular criminal any more, their focus has changed."

"What are you going to do? Kate said.

"I will never give up until we get him, even if I have to do it myself. Someday, he will pay!" Jacob said.

"It's going to be good to get away for a couple of days," Kate said.

"When I am with you it is always my best day."

Jacob and Kate woke that next morning excited to be together at one of their favorite places. They enjoyed walking the beach; Kate enjoyed finding unusual pieces of driftwood for her art projects. They liked watching Blu, their Alaskan malamute, run crazy up and down the beach. Occasionally, a surprise would wash up on the beach after a storm for them to talk about.

Jacob woke first and lit the camp stove for their morning coffee and let Blu out of the tent, Blu sprinted off toward the water. Jacob noticed a funny smell in the air. He did not think too much about it. He and Kate sipped coffee and planned out their day.

Jacob kept calling Blu, he did not respond. He was down by the water sniffing something.

"What is Blu doing?" Kate said.

"He is more interested in what is down there than us," Jacob said.

Before they reached the water's edge, they saw what Blu was captivated by.

"No! Damn it, no! This can't be happening!" Jacob yelled.

Chapter 25

Vladimir started up the ramp to the green colored ship. A crew member standing at the top of the ramp yelled out-are you Mr. Kozlov?

"Yes, I am," Vladimir replied.

"Come aboard and let me show you to your bunk, then a tour of the ship and introduction to the captain and crew," Tony said.

"Great, I can't wait to get started," Vladimir said.

Tony led Vladimir to a bunk and introduced him to a couple of crew members along the way. Vladimir tossed his pack on his bunk and turned toward Tony.

"Is there a computer I might be able to use once all the introductions are done?" Vladimir said.

"Yes, there is Mr. Kozlov. Let's go meet the captain, and then I will set you up on a computer."

The captain was a short, chubby, bearded man. He had a smile on his face to greet Vladimir. His weak hand shake left Vladimir confident.

"I want to thank you for that generous donation," Captain Dobbs said.

"You are welcome; your organization does some great work," Vladimir said.

"We are going north toward Alaska to monitor the whale migration; it should give you plenty of time on board to see what we do and how we do it."

"Thank you."

"Tony will be your guide throughout the trip Mr. Kozlov," Captain Dobbs said.

"Great, thank you again, Captain,"

"Oh, last thing, we have a plane ticket waiting for you in Anchorage. That will be as far as we can take you Mr. Kozlov."

"That was more than I was expecting Captain, thank you sir."

"What would you like to do first Mr. Kozlov?" Tony said.

"If you don't mind, I would like to rest for a short time."

"Ok I will be in the communications room next to the helm, when you're ready just come and get me."

"I will do that," Vladimir said.

Vladimir called Dmitri once the ship left the docks. "Dmitri, I am leaving the docks as we speak, we are heading north toward Anchorage, follow us from a distance, you can't miss the ship, it is green with a rainbow on the front."

"We will start north now," Dmitri said.

"Call Pavel and let him know where we'll be," Vladimir said.

"Ok, we see you soon," Dmitri said.

Vladimir didn't wait long before he strolled down the hall to the communications room. He opened the door to find it empty. No Tony or any crew member. The computer was on. This will be easier. he thought. I have to risk it.

He sat and started his search, looking in every shortcut on the computer desktop for the information; there must have been dozens of them. Vladimir clicked on a few short cuts before he heard someone speaking outside the door. He powered down the computer, closed the top and leaned back, his hands clenched behind his head as Tony walked in.

"Hey Mr. Kozlov, I've been looking for you," Tony said.

"I've been wondering around, decided to wait for you in here," Vladimir said.

"Is there anything in particular you would like to see first?" Tony said.

"Yes, from what I understand you study many things including climate change, the health of the forests, and oceans, are you trying to protect the whales from extinction, the whale situation sounds like a good place to start, how do you prevent the whales from getting slaughtered by the fleet of whalers?"

"Good question. The Japanese and Russians are the biggest threat to the whales in the Pacific, even more now than in the past. The worldwide food shortage is creating chaos. They are becoming desperate for food in those countries and are willing to break any treaty or invade our waters."

"Wow, sounds like an impossible task," Vladimir said.

"We have a satellite tracking system helping us monitor many whale groups; it makes a big difference, knowing where all these groups of whales are at any given time," Tony said.

"That is amazing – can I see you tracking a whale now?"

"Yes, come over to the computer and I will show you."

Vladimir watched every step as Tony opened the satellite tracking program. As the main page opened, Vladimir noticed, starting on the top of the page and working down the page were names, followed by radio frequencies. Vladimir screamed inside his head. He found the mother lode, all the information he needed. He counted down the page, forty-eight different names and frequencies. He was surprised, that they had more whales tagged than they had advertised to the public.

Tony opened up the first one on the list, and up popped a map showing the exact location the whale last surfaced. The map showed the whole route the whale was on. There was a red dot each time the whale surfaced, displaying the longitude and latitude and the direction it was going.

"That is a great system; can you show me around the rest of the ship now?

"Yes, let's go."

After the tour of the ship, Vladimir went back to his bunk and started planning his next move. He had Dmitri following close by and Pavel a day or two away. He needed remote access to tracking system where those coordinates would be found and the pass word was the only way to get into the system. He waited until late night, most of the crew had long disappeared to their bunks, and then he made his move to the computer room.

The computer was still on; the prompt was blinking, waiting for an input into the satellite tracking system. Vladimir entered the password he seen Tony use, anticipating he was about to win again. The program fired up. Vladimir connected his laptop to theirs and proceeded to download the complete tracking program and satellite information.

Vladimir kept peeking out the door, his 9mm in hand. Sweat pooled on his forehead, and his heart raced as the download trickled on. Less than an hour later, the download was complete. Vladimir unplugged the computer and returned to his bunk. He packed the laptop computer and his 9mm into his pack and rapped them with his clothes.

The ocean was peaceful, the dark night faded as Vladimir entered the helm. "Hello, Mr. Kozlov, how was your tour of the ship?" the captain said.

"It was great, I need to get to Crescent city ASAP! Vladimir said.

"Why, what's wrong? The captain said.

"It's my daughter, she was in a car accident, I need to see her right away,"

"It will be hours before we can get you there."

"She is in intensive care; she might not make it."

"Tony, get the helicopter ready," the captain said.

"Captain, I don't know how I can thank you," Vladimir said.

* * * *

The helicopter touched down before noon on a flat piece of dirt above Crescent city. Vladimir waved off the pilot. He raised his fist up in the air in victory as the chopper turned into a dot far out to sea.

Vladimir immediately called Dmitri on his satellite phone, Dmitri was quick to answer... "Dmitri, come and pick me up in Crescent City; let's finish this and get filthy rich."

Vladimir walked chest out down to the small harbor. He sat on an old rotting bench at the end of the pier and waited for Dmitri. He turned on the computer and studied the tracking program. He was confident this would be his biggest score yet.

The harbor had a familiar look to it; it brought back some old memories of his past life in Russia. Chills covered Vladimir's body, and his stomach churned, a sharp pain jolted his brain, thinking about what happened to his wife back in Russia. Both their lives ended that day; guilt invaded his soul. He pounded the old wooden bench, until it was just a pile of rotting sticks. He stared at the rotted wood for a few seconds as he backed up to the other side of the pier looking in all directions, hoping he was not seen. Not long after Vladimir spotted a ship. Dmitri was cruising toward the harbor, and it shook Vladimir back to the current reality and cut him loose of his anger and self-pity.

Vladimir's confidence grew, seeing Dmitri pull into the harbor. He untied a small row boat from the dock and rowed out to meet him and his crew.

"We have everything we need Dmitri, are you ready to become rich?" Vladimir said.

"We are ready, we have a great ship and crew, not so sure about the old rust bucket Pavel is bringing," Dmitri said.

"I personally checked it out and made sure it was seaworthy; you are going to love the modifications I made on it," Vladimir said.

"I hope so, this whole operation depends on the rust bucket," Dmitri said.

"Trust me, it's ok, did you tell Pavel where to meet us?" Vladimir said.

"Yeah, he will be there tomorrow," Dmitri said.

"Good, let's get going, we have some work to do before he shows up," Vladimir said.

Vladimir had the tracking program up and running and had all the whales' radio frequency IDs on screen. He plotted a course to intercept. The system was even better than he was hoping for.

Vladimir and crew headed north, directly in the path of the migration. It was not long before they seen whales breach the water in the exact spot the tracking system showed they would be.

"We are going to be rich," Dmitri said, as multiple whales breached the water.

"Once we meet up with Pavel and the rust bucket, we will be rich, let's get ahead of them, full steam ahead," Vladimir said.

The ship motored north a couple of hours and a huge payday, for an unknown reason to Vladimir, the crew started firing into the water, the men screamed and laughed as they shot their sniper rifles wildly into the water.

"Let's go see what those idiots are shooting at," Vladimir said.

Vladimir and Dmitri rushed to the front of the ship.

"A little target practice?" Vladimir said.

"Yes boss, just having some fun," the crew men said.

"Let me see your gun," Vladimir said.

The crewmen handed Vladimir his rifle. Vladimir fired off the remaining bullets in the clip and put in another. He laughed as he fired, killing everything within range. Vladimir stopped firing, he glared over at the crew man who fired first and shot him in the leg and continued firing until the clip was empty. He pushed the bloodless dead man over board and threw the gun to Dmitri.

"Someone mop the deck!" Vladimir said. The other men stood there in shock, frozen in time, no one wanting to move or show any emotion for fear they'd be next.

"We cannot afford to draw attention to us by shooting fish that we can't even make a profit on," Vladimir said... "Those dolphins might be chasing down bait fish and our prize will not be far behind them. That man was reckless and would get us all killed. He had to go; do you men want to die for a fool like that? This is not fun and games, get back to work!" The crew dispersed without a word and went to work getting ready for the chase.

"Keep following those dolphins, I have seen this before, the whales will be going to the same location, if they are after a bait ball," Vladimir said.

As the sun set, Vladimir and his crew met up with Pavel and the old rust bucket off the Oregon Coast and waited. Once the tracking system was up and running, they set the ship directly in the path of three separate RF signals.

Chapter 26

Kate lips tightened; Jacob covered his mouth with his fist. They stared in disbelief seeing them. Over twenty of them, some of them still alive. They approached one that was still moving and tried to help it, only to have it die minutes later. They ran over to another that was still breathing, but bleeding from its head.

Kate applied pressure to the wound. The dolphin peered directly into her eyes, and made a short chirp. Kate took a deep breath, her lips tightened, fist clenched. The dolphin struggled to breathe, its eyes closed, then nothing. Not another breath, it died with Kate still holding pressure on the wound, Tears pooled and rolled down her cheeks. She didn't want to let go.

"This is heartbreaking, who would do something like this?" Kate said.

"Things like this have been on the increase; mostly it's been done for food. This, though, has the look of pure evil, killing for the sake of killing," Jacob said.

Jacob and Kate went to every dolphin on the beach; they were all shot in the head area and all were dead or would be soon.

"Whoever shot these dolphins is an expert marksman; each one is a head shot; only an expert marksman is that precise."

"Should we call the police or your company?" Kate said.

"Yeah, I will make a call to both, in the meantime I know of a boat a few miles from here. Let's get out of here; I need to get to the boat and recon the area for information on who might have done this," Jacob said.

"Can I go with you?"

"I don't think so; this could be dangerous if I run into someone."

"You can't go by yourself."

"I don't have a choice," Jacob said.

"Please don't go alone, please let me go with you."

Jacob was hesitant in his response. Going alone was risky but bringing Kate was out of the question; the risk was too high. What if he had one of his JOB moments out there; he would not be able to live with himself if something happened to her.

"I can't take you with me Kate."

"Why?"

"Xian is a few hours away; he will help me out on the water. I need you to do something else for me."

"Anything, what do you need.?"

"I need you to find the names of the big donors who contributed to the Congressmen's Campaign,"

"What does that have to do with anything that's going on now?"

"I have some suspicions about the donors," Jacob said.

"You are just trying to get rid of me."

"No, I think there might be a connection, I didn't want to tell you, I might be unemployed soon. Your congressman is pushing to close us down and at the worst possible time. It just doesn't make any sense."

"That is strange, he claims to be this environmentalist. Yeah, I will find out why, what else should I look for?" Kate said.

"Something feels wrong, the timing of all this is suspect, find out what are they getting in return for the money, who they are, and why they are contributing so much at this time," Jacob said.

Jacob kissed Kate and closed the door. He touched his chest with his fist and ran toward the office. Kate and Blu left Jacob at the dock and headed for home. She was excited about spying for Jacob; she was curious about these large donations also.

* * * *

Jacob stopped at the front door, a sign in the window, *Closed*. He turned the door knob, it was locked. Waiting for the owner to show up was not an option. He broke the window and entered. Jacob knew where the owner, a close friend, had his guns, Jacob used a sledgehammer to pound the lock off the safe. The guns were in a safe as expected, a 9mm handgun and extra loaded clips plus an AR15. He found the extra set of keys for his boat in a family friend's boat, docked in the slip next to his.

Jacob fired up the engine to his cruiser, set the AR15, the 9mm handgun and extra clips on the seat, and headed west. Before he left the dock, he made the call to Xian. Xian had made it to Seattle and was on board the 80-foot *Sea Breeze* heading south. This was one of two ships that INECE had on the west coast used for enforcement. There was no doubt what this boat was for. It was set up with all the electronics needed for tracking illegal activity on the sea and the fifty caliber on the bow let everybody know the ship was there for business.

"Do you have anything on Vladimir?" Jacob asked.

"No nothing of where he might be now," Xian replied.

"I came across the brutal killing of about thirty dolphins on the beach here in Oregon; we need to pursue this first until we find out more about where Vladimir is," Jacob said.

"Where do you want to meet?"

"Head down the coast toward our old stomping grounds, the beach in Oregon where we had the trouble with the jellyfish back in college. I need to find out who did this."

"See you in a couple of hours."

Jacob raced the cruiser south, as the sun was starting to set. It wasn't long before he made it to the area of the dolphin killing, he sighted a large ship off the starboard bow. The odd shaped ship seemed out of place and dated.

Jacob wanted to investigate the odd ship. It would have to wait. He was determined to find out who killed the dolphins. This is the exact reason Jacob joined INECE, to catch ruthless criminals who had no regard for the ecosystem and the planet.

He stopped half mile off shore from the beach where he and Kate found the dead and dying dolphins. There was not much to see as the days light melted away. There was a lot of activity and squawking on the beach from the birds scavenging on the dead carcasses. The only thing Jacob could see in the absence of light, where the lights from a ship, miles to the west.

Jacob had seen nothing on the way south to indicate criminal behavior. He had no other options; he checked his fuel gauge and turned west toward a light fading in and out of sight.

Chapter 27

Pavel met up with Vladimir just as the sun went down. He ordered Pavel to follow him northwest the same direction as a handful of dolphins were headed. As the dolphins started to feed, he had Pavel and the old rust bucket set up almost on top of the feeding dolphins. There they waited for the money haul. Vladimir intensely monitored the computer screen. The tracking system worked to perfection. They were heading right toward them.

"I am a genius, this is working even better than I imagined it would," Vladimir said.

"I will contact Pavel and have the men ready on the bow of the rust bucket," Dmitri said.

"Yeah, make sure their locked and loaded," Vladimir said.

Vladimir monitored the computer closely, and as the direction of the signal changed, he ordered Pavel to move the rust bucket to keep in line with the pod of whales. The signals were getting close to their location, within a couple hundred meters from where the rust bucket was floating.

"They will be within range soon, make sure the men are ready." Vladimir said.

The five men were ready on the bow. All were lined up in a semi-circle about ten feet apart and perched five feet off the deck. Each man, poised with his finger on the trigger waited for the word. Vladimir sat a short distance away on the 45-foot fishing boat.

"Turn on the floodlights and get ready, they're almost there!" Vladimir yelled from the loudspeaker.

The swells off the bow of the rust bucket increased. The men took aim and waited for a breach; a large male humpback surfaced first. Shots rang out, multiple whales continued to breach the cold waters of the pacific. The five-foot long harpoons were straight and on target. Each penetrated the whale with tremendous force. Three more simultaneous breaches and three more harpoons were launched flying through the air with enough force to penetrate deep into the whale's flesh, all harpoons made direct hits, the humpbacks struggled to dive but were unable to go to deep, as the ropes were tied off to the rust bucket.

The harpoons were connected to steel cables connected to heavy duty winches. The whales dove numerous times, only making it down ten feet or less, and then resurfaced.

Vladimir and Dmitri raced over to the thrashing whales. They stopped six feet away. Vladimir unloaded his powerful six shot revolver into the head of the first whale. Dmitri moved the fishing boat in range of the next whale. Vladimir again unloaded six shots to the head of the next helpless whale. The men on the rust bucket cheered as he methodically unloaded his revolver into each whale as it surfaced.

The water turned red with blood, one by one the thrashing whales floated on the surface dead. The only movement were two calves, who would not leave their mother's side.

The harpooners slid the cables along the side of the rust bucket to the stern and one by one the whales floated to the stern as the rust bucket moved forward. There they attached a rope around the tail and pulled it up the ramp to the top flat deck with another winch, for gutting and butchering. One after another the humpbacks were pulled up the ramp to the deck of the rust bucket.

The calves followed as the whales were pulled to the stern. The calves swam to the back of the ramp and rested their heads on the bottom of the open ramp. As each Humpback was pulled up to the top deck; blood drained the ramp into the water. The dark red blood encircled the calves, as they watched.

As the last whale was pulled to the deck, Vladimir called to Pavel and had two of the ropes lowered to the bottom of the ramp.

"Dmitri, get me over to the stern of the rust bucket, fast," Vladimir said.

Dmitri pulled the fishing boat to the stern; carefully maneuvered it between the two calves. Vladimir jumped from the fishing boat onto the rust bucket. He retrieved two ropes and handed them over to a crew man on the fishing boat.

They roped the tail of the calves as they rested their heads on the ramp of the Rust bucket. Vladimir retrieved the ropes and had his men connect them to the winches. He ordered his men to shoot the water behind the calves.

The calves dove and disappeared into the bloody water. The slack in the ropes tightened around their tails as they dove deeper. They violently thrashed as they were pulled to the surface.

"We have them; pull them up to where the others are being butchered," Vladimir said.

"What is that noise?" Dmitri yelled.

"What noise?" Vladimir said.

"Listen," Dmitri said.

Chapter 28

The only thing Jacob saw on the water was a single light from a ship in the distance. He steered toward the faint light into the vast blackness of the Pacific. The closer Jacob got, the more he realized something was not right. The light illuminated more of the monster ship as he advanced. He approached with caution, using his binoculars to assess the situation.

"I got you; you will not escape this time Vladimir; you will pay for all your crimes."

Jacob's fists tightened around the steering wheel, and his jaw clenched tight. He threw caution out the window. *This is going to be crazy, I don't see any other options, and if I wait for help, they will disappear into the vastness of the Pacific.*

He opened up the two front windows, picked up the AR15 with his left hand and the 9mm with his right. He raced full throttle toward the old factory ship. The bow of his boat bounced up and down, pounding the water as it cascaded over the bow, flooding the wheelhouse and drenching him with salty frigid water. Jacob's eyes burned, as he headed for the stern of the ship.

Jacob buried the throttle. The boat plowed through the water, the pointed bow rose high off the surface and pounded deep into the ocean, spraying water, port and starboard. He started to fire his AR15 at the fishing boat at the rear of the whaling ship. The men on the ship froze, before they scrambled for cover. Jacob crashed into the bow of the fishing boat, pushing it aside as he fired. His cruiser slid up the ramp of the factory ship and stopped feet from the Humpback calves on the ramp. He turned off the engine and lowered the prop all the way down so as not to slide down the ramp back into the water.

Jacob's bold move put the poachers into complete disarray. He turned to fire on the fishing boat, but it was gone. He fired at the men on the factory ship, and they all ducked for cover. He stood on the bow of his boat aiming his AR15 up toward the deck. There was no return fire. He stood and shouted, "I work for law enforcement, you are all under arrest!"

Jacob jumped from the bow onto the ramp of the factory ship. He crawled up the blood-soaked ramp to the calves. He soon realized they were still alive. Their eyes focused on Jacob, as he touched them. They watched every move he made.

He crawled up toward the rope wrapped around the tails of the calves. He latched onto a rope just as his boat slid down the ramp and crashing into the water. It did not stop at the bottom of the ramp; it kept floating farther and farther away from the factory ship. He had a choice; go after his boat now or save these calves.

God, why do these things happen to me?

Jacob turned and glanced into the calves' eyes; the eyes made the choice for him. He cut the rope to one calf, and it made a strange noise, as it slid down the ramp into the water. He started to cut the rope for the second calf, but men with automatic weapons opened fire from the wheelhouse.

Jacob crawled up the ramp, soaked in the blood from the gutted humpbacks. The deck covered in whales and end trails, left little room for Jacob to stand upright. He stood on the deck of the factory ship with AR15 in hand, ready to shut this operation down. He moved toward the wheelhouse screaming you are all under arrest. Not surprising, he was greeted with gun fire. Jacob was shocked by the fire power that was thrust upon him.

Jacob fired off the remaining rounds in his AR15 and dove for cover onto the deck. The blood and guts from the whales still spewed on the deck covered him. Bullets flew everywhere. He had nowhere to go and was trapped, he had no choice and rolled off the deck into a gutted humpback.

Jacob slid deep into the belly of the whale. The opening ran from head to tail. Heavy thumps vibrated the whale blubber, Jacob moved deeper into the carcass. He gagged a few times and almost let loose breakfast.

The bullets never reached him, only penetrating the thick blubber of the whale. Jacob fired off an occasional round from his 9mm just to let them know he was still alive. He was protected but doubted it would long; he had to get off the ship while it was still dark. Jacob had to make a move; the poachers would overpower him soon.

Jacob recognized, they left large thick chunks of blubber on deck next to the carcass. He crawled through blood, bone, blubber and the stench to get to the head of the whale, which was closest to the ramp. He peeked out of the carcass. No shots were fired. He dove onto a piece of blubber. The men from the wheelhouse started firing as he slid down the ramp on a large piece of blubber. He fired off another round floating in the cold water of the Pacific on a five-foot long, three-feet thick piece of whale blubber.

He rolled off the raft of blubber and submerged beneath, as he was fired on. Holding tight onto the blubber, he kicked himself and the raft out of the illuminated waters of the ship's lights and into the Pacific. Once the firing stopped, he rolled back onto the raft, lying flat on his back out of the freezing water. He gazed up to heaven shivering, shaking his head side to side. *What did I get myself into, another test?*

Jacob let the current take him away from the ship, hoping it would take him close to wherever his boat was. As he floated away from the ship, Jacob could see the outline of the fishing boat he rammed; it was listing to its port side. Jacob overheard the men on the fishing boat talking. Then came the name he was hoping to hear- –

Vladimir! Hearing his name angered and at the same time gave him happiness.

They were a short distance from the factory ship, far enough away to be out of the lights of the ship, and into the dark. Jacob was hoping they were too busy trying not to sink and would not see him as he floated past on the raft of blubber. A loud voice spoke-

"Get us back to the ship so we can check on our damage – we need to find and kill that man,"

* * * *

Vladimir pulled up to the stern of the factory ship and

tied off. The damage to the bow on his boat was cracked, but it was still sea worthy.

"Pavel, what's going on, there was a lot of gunfire? Vladimir said.

Pavel leaned over the railing. "He said he was the law. We had a shootout and forced him back in the water, he is either dead or floating out there somewhere, but not for long, hypothermia will set in fast."

Vladimir boarded the rust bucket. "Go search for him and his boat and see if he is still alive."

His men idled away on the fishing boat in search of the law man.

Chapter 29

Jacob didn't see any sign of his boat. He was freezing; his hands and feet were numb. Jacob would not last much longer floating on the water-logged raft. He had to find his boat. It was out there somewhere but how far away and which direction was just a guess. He stopped paddling and kicking and floated to analyze the direction of the currents.

Jacob watched as their spotlight scanned the water but never came close to him. After an hour of searching, they gave up. He had to find his boat before daybreak or he would be dead. Jacob's only other option, go back to the factory ship and hide out.

Jacob had spent too much time in the frigid water and with no sighting of his boat, he made a choice. He started paddling back toward the ship while it was still dark. His MTM Seal Watch read an hour before he reached the factory ship. Jacob relaxed a bit, his heart no longer pounded into his chest. Before his heart pumped normal, there was violent shaking of the raft. Back and forth it went. A cold sweat invaded every part of his body, his heart raced. His nightmare was inches away.

The small shark ripped at the side of the three-foot-thick piece of blubber. Jacob froze.

His worst fear was in his face. The shark bit down on his raft, it's black eyes broke into Jacob's soul.

"God help me," Jacob mumbled.

The shark tore at the edge the blubber.

Not long after Jacob's prayer, the shaking stopped. The shark turned and disappeared with a chunk of blubber protruding from its jaws.

"Thank GOD." The raft still afloat. He feverously paddled toward the ship. The closer to the ship he got, his heavy breathing and heart beat slowed. He wanted to shout something, anything, to release the built-up tension. Feet from safety, the violent shaking started again. The shaking was so violent; he was tossed off the raft.

The shark tore off another piece of blubber and disappeared. His raft began to sink. He had no choice. Jacob jumped from the raft and swam like never before.

With every stroke, Jacob thought he was going to die; he powered through the water, his entire body ended up on the ramp of the factory ship. Jacob exhausted, struggled for air. He crawled up the ramp, away from the water.

He lay on the bottom of the ramp gasping for air. The water behind the ship was agitated, his raft was viciously ripped apart by numerous sharks. He lay on the ramp shivering; his hands and feet numb. The large fishing boat searching for him was a half mile away, it was not an immediate concern. He had to find some place to hide on the ship before day break.

The ramp was steep and slippery. He grasped on to a small gap on the side of the ramp with finger tips, he lodged his boots into the narrow gap but did not hold. He crawled on his stomach toward the deck; only his finger tips holding from slipping. Jacob struggled up a couple of feet, lost his grip, and slid back down into the water. After a few tries of getting nowhere, he lay at the bottom of the ramp frustrated and stuck. His legs were forced into the water. He kicked, keeping his body from entering fully, he was not going back into the water even as a last resort.

There were still two things working in his favor. The crewmen had not seen him yet and his 9mm had two rounds left. Looking at the 9mm gave him an idea that might just get him out of this mess. Jacob removed the clip from the gun and jammed the hammer into the small gap in the ramp. It stuck and held. Jacob pulled himself up the ramp a foot at a time.

Halfway up the slippery blood-stained ramp he rested. The steepest section of the ramp was now ahead of him. As Jacob started up Everest, the ship's engines started to turn the propellers. The ship moved forward. Rolling side to side, the ramp was even tougher to climb. "What else could go wrong?" Jacob mumbled.

Jacob struggled to crawl up the steep section of the ramp; he removed the hammer of the gun and slid back down the ramp a couple of feet before it dug in and caught. He kept sliding back in this same steep section; he had to try something else. All Jacob had left to use was the clip. With the clip in one hand the gun in the other; hand over hand; he jammed each in the small opening and inched his way to the top of the deck.

Jacob noticed two wooden lifeboats propped up behind some equipment on the starboard side, they were covered with dirty canvas tarps some forty feet away.

The crewmen were scattered on the large ship; making it to the lifeboat unseen did not seem like a problem.

The ship headed northeast as Jacob settled into the lifeboat. He peeked out and monitored the movement of the men on deck. They were all busy doing something; some were cutting up the whale meat, others were working on the ship and some walking the deck watching the ocean with binoculars. The number of poachers left Jacob doubtful he would be successful by himself.

Jacob laid low in the lifeboat, peeking out as men with binoculars and AK-74s walked the ship studying the ocean. Jacob checked his watch, hoping Xian would be getting close. The lifeboat suddenly shook; he held his breath and froze. Someone was there, he was ready with his pistol, he had one bullet in his chamber and one bullet in his pocket, the clip was bent beyond use. Jacob was relieved, he smelled cigarette smoke.

Jacob set his gun down and peeked out the tarp; the man was standing inches from him. He was staring at the back of his head; without hesitation he reached out and put the man in a choke hold. His grip was strong; he chocked the man unconscious and pulled him into the life boat. He gagged and tied the man up using rope and the straps from a life vest and laid him face down.

One down, Jacob thought.

He peeked out from under the tarp; things were calm on deck. The crewman started to move after a minute; Jacob held his pistol to his head.

"You will answer my questions or I will toss you overboard, many sharks out there, do you understand?"

Jacob said.

The man nodded.

Jacob removed the gag and shoved the gun against his forehead. "How many men are on board?"

"Twelve," the crewman mumbled.

Jacob put the gag back in and tied him face down to the floor board. While Jacob interrogated his prisoner the ship stopped. The deck became alive. Someone from the wheelhouse was yelling out orders, sometimes in Russian, sometimes in English. It didn't take long for Jacob to know who was barking out orders from the wheelhouse.

What Jacob saw next confused him. The men hoisted the baby calf over the railing and dropped it back into the water. The ship was backed away, and they positioned the bow facing the humpback calf. The calf pounded its tail violently on the water trying to escape the rope tied around it. Jacob's anger was growing by the second watching this brutal event.

* * * *

"We are now sitting on the coordinates for a tagged killer whale. They can be found in groups so this will be very lucrative if my plan works," Vladimir said.

"We don't have much time before daybreak; do you think we can get it done before then? Dmitri said.

"Yeah, we will have them on board and be on our way before daybreak," Vladimir said.

"What time are we meeting our buyers?" Dmitri said.

"They should be on board sometime tomorrow around midnight," Vladimir said.

"With all this meat we have, it will show them what we are capable of," Dmitri said.

"The way things are in the world today, not even a game warden or whoever he was will be able to stop us," Vladimir said.

"This next kill should be very lucrative," Dmitri said.

"It will be, but first we need to have the meat on board, butchered and on ice before the buyers get here. We have a lot of work to do before we can start counting our money," Vladimir said.

"Where are we going after we off load this haul?" Dmitri said.

"The Arctic Circle is next. If everything goes as planned up there, we will be able to retire and live the life of millionaires – once all the whales are on board, get the ship headed for our meeting location with our American buyers," Vladimir said.

"Ok boss," Dmitri said.

Chapter 30

Jacob could only see the starboard side of the bow from the life boat. He had to get closer. He made sure his prisoner was secured and exited the life boat. Jacob hid behind two other life boats and some metal containers on his way to the bow.

What Jacob saw on the bow was even worse than he expected. The factory ship was equipped with five high-powered harpoons. All five had the look of death and powerful enough to sink a ship if need be. They were killing tools. The men operating them were ready on the trigger, eyes focused on the whale calf, illuminated by the ship's floodlights.

"They are close and coming right for the calf," a Russian spoke over the speaker.

The ship backed away from the trashing calf and waited thirty feet away. The men were ready with fingers on trigger. As expected, out of the depths, a tall black intimidating fin broke the surface of the water. The fin circled the calf and then three others broke the surface and circled.

Jacob watched from behind a container in total disbelief. He never wanted to believe someone, even Vladimir, could be so cruel. The calf had stopped trashing and floated on the surface, the poachers were fast and with violent precision. Jacob watched two simultaneous strikes from the killer whales, one to the head and one to the tail. The calf was silent and two more strikes to the belly, ended it.

Disgusted, Jacob took a deep breath, his fists clenched tight. His anger put him in go mode. He was ready to take them all to jail after seeing this horrific tragedy. To make it worse, he saw them commit another atrocity. They fired the harpoons as each whale surfaced to feed on the dead calf. All hit their mark. The five harpoons penetrated deep into the flesh of the killer whales.

Three of the whales were killed instantly with harpoons to the head. The remaining two struggled to escape. There was no escape and they floated to the surface lifeless, with a large harpoon embedded in their flesh.

Jacob had seen enough. His anger boiled over; he took deep breaths and headed back to the lifeboat to think about his next move. Once he was in the lifeboat, he remembered a passage he once read, Psalms 37:20 – "but the wicked shall perish, and the enemies of the lord shall be as the fat as lambs: they shall consume; into smoke shall they consume away."

This gave him calm, as he thought about his next move. He needed more information from his prisoner. He lifted the poacher off the floor and held his pistol to his head while he removed the gag from his mouth.

"What you guys are doing here is not only a serious crime, it's inhumane," Jacob said. "Do you understand how your greed is destroying these animals?"

"I just wanted a job; I didn't know how far Vladimir would go," the Russian said.

"So, Vladimir is the leader of this lawless group."

"Yeah, I never thought he would go to this extreme, he is out of control, he even killed a close friend of mine."

"Tell me – and do not BS me… how many men are on board?"

The prisoner looked down, hesitated… "twelve and two more are on the other fishing boat."

"Who are the buyers for this meat?"

There was another long pause by the prisoner. His answer shocked Jacob. "I don't know their names, but they are from America. They will be onboard tomorrow to buy the meat."

"Perfect, I will stop all these lawless criminals tomorrow!"

"I will help you if you let me," the prisoner said.

"You want me to trust you? You must be related to that mad man Vladimir if you think I would trust you," Jacob said.

"I never thought he would go this far."

"Tell me what you know about him."

"He was in the military until they threw him in jail."

"What was his crime?"

"He killed a bunch of people who were protesting against the government in Kazan."

"That event corrupted him and turned him into a sociopath?" Jacob said.

"There was a rumor that his wife and child were killed in that same incident in Moscow."

"Are you saying he was responsible for their deaths?"

"That's the rumor," the Russian said.

Disgusted, Jacob shoved the man to the deck and tightened the gag around his mouth. Jacob wanted this stopped here and now, it could not continue. If they cashed in on this haul, with this ship and its capabilities they would be millionaires and would disappear for good. This would be his last chance to get this killer and his crew.

Jacob watched as the first killer whale was pulled up the ramp. Once the whale was on the deck, the Flenser inserted the blade and slit the belly all the way to the head as it was being pulled forward by the winch. Then the rest of the men went to work. The Lemmers and blubber boys worked with precision, cutting the blubber and meat into smaller pieces and then it was stored below deck on ice. Within a short time, all the killer whales were on board and being butchered.

While all the men were at work, Jacob made his move. He put on the jacket and hat of his prisoner and jumped down onto the deck with the AK-74 at his side. He pulled the hat down over his face and causally walked toward the bow on the starboard side, avoiding the lights as much as possible. He stopped behind a container where the lights of the ship did not reach. His target was twenty feet away, Jacob waved him over. Jacob turned his back to the man as he approached.

"What do you want?" he asked.

"You," Jacob said. He pounded the butt end of the AK-74 into the man's forehead. The man went down with the side of his face hitting the deck hard. He laid there unconscious with blood pouring from his nose. Jacob walked up toward the bow staying in the dark behind the containers. He peered around the last container, on the bow another target smoking a cigarette.

Jacob whistled to get his attention. The man turned toward him blowing smoke from his mouth. Jacob waved him over to the container. Jacob ducked behind the container. The crewman followed and Jacob slammed the butt of his AK-74 into his stomach and two quick blows to the face. The man was stunned and stumbled but did not go down. His eyes opened wide seeing Jacob's face. He started to raise his AK-74, but Jacob hit him again.

The crewman lunged at Jacob. He became familiar with the butt of the rifle to his forehead. The Russian planted his face on the deck with a loud *thump*. Blood pooled around the poacher's head. Relieved, Jacob scanned around the ship; with everyone still working on the whales, he had not been noticed.

Jacob dragged the man back to the other crewman who was still unconscious. He gagged the new man and tied them both with some rope he found next to the container. Jacob pulled both men to the lifeboat and hoisted them inside. He crawled in and secured them to the wooden seats and went back to the container to recover their AK-74s.

Jacob sat in the lifeboat with his three prisoners, peeking out to study the men working on the deck. The deck was almost clear; the last of the meat was being stored below deck.

Jacob recognized the lifeboat was connected to a hoist; it gave him an idea. He scanned the deck again from the front of the lifeboat; there was only one man left, and he was busy cleaning the blood-stained wooden deck. Every other crewman had gone below deck.

Another opportunity presented itself; he had to avoid being seen by someone in the wheelhouse for it to work. Darkness and surprise were in his favor, the men in the wheelhouse were busy. He made his move.

Jacob disguised in the poacher's hat and jacket, casually strolled over to a crewman cleaning the deck. He looked up with a smile on his face, his smile turned to big eyed stare. Jacob shoved his pistol to his head.

"Get moving or I will shoot you right here, right now," Jacob said.

The man did not put up a fight. Jacob had him tied up and secured in the lifeboat without much trouble. Jacob stood a little taller, his chest puffed out, his confidence building as things were going his way. He needed more information.

The gag was removed from the deck swabber's mouth and a pistol put to his head.

"How many men are on board?" Jacob asked.

The man would not answer. Jacob smacked him on the bridge of the nose with the pistol but, still no answer. The man, bleeding profusely from his nose on to his beard, sat and said nothing.

"Look you have two choices; you can tell me what I want to know or you can go swimming, what will it be?

The man still did not talk.

"If I have to drag you from this lifeboat you are going over pal, there is no return."

The man sat there with this arrogant look on his face and said nothing.

"Ok criminal, that's the way it's going to be."

Jacob smashed the man in the mouth with the butt of his pistol and put gag back in his mouth and pushed him out of the lifeboat onto the deck. He picked the man up and leaned him on the railing.

"You and your boss Vladimir have killed and hurt some of my closet friends, so dumping you over the side is justified in my mind, I don't have a problem with it," Jacob said.

Jacob lifted the man up over the railing, his prisoner mumbled "stop, stop!"

"Did I hear you right?"

The prisoner shook his head in agreement. He opened up like a mountain spring, spilling its water onto the ground. Jacob received all the information from his prisoner and then some.

He pushed his prisoner back into the life boat and went to the hoist controls. He raised the lifeboat off the deck and maneuvered it over the railing, watching the wheelhouse as he lowered it into the water. He cut the old rope holding the stern a foot above the water and he cut the last rope connected to the bow, the lifeboat drifted away from the factory ship. *I'll deal with you killers later.*

Jacob had no time to waste. Soon they would realize there was a missing lifeboat and crewmen. Jacob headed to the back of the ship and entered the first door he came to. There was a metal stairway leading down toward the stern. Halfway down the stairs he found a hatch to his right, and at the bottom was another door. He opened the hatch which led to a steel walkway above the engine room and ended on the opposite side of the ship at another hatch. He walked down to the door at the bottom of the stairs. Jacob leaned on the door; he held on for dear life as it popped open with ease, almost falling into the Pacific, there was metal rebar used for steps leading to the waterline. *Damn, if I would have known these steps were here.* He saw a similar door, possibility leading to the water on the other side of the ship.

Jacob hurried back up the stairs and reopened the hatch; he saw it was clear. He hid one of the AKs outside the hatch under one of the stairs and entered the metal cat walk. He opened the door on the opposite side, and a nasty smell overtook him, flooding his nostrils with a stench of death; it was so bad his eyes burned.

Jacob covered his nose and entered. It was dark and cold; he could see the ice and something else from what little light that entered through the hatch.

I did not think things could get worse than the whale calf being used as bait, but this tops it. These ruthless military killers might be more than I can handle alone.

Jacob stared in disbelief, his face heated, the mystery smell revealed itself. His hatred toward the poachers grew by the second. But he knew anger and hatred was not going to solve this tragedy. God willing, he would, somehow.

Jacob closed the hatch, but not before he hid another AK in the room filled with death. He started down the stairs toward the noisy engines and paused. Two men walked up to the engines. They stood there and talked for a few minutes, then both engines shut down. Jacob backed up the stairs as the men started to work on the engines. He laid face down on the metal catwalk and crawled to the other side.

Jacob made it unseen across the walk and opened the hatch. Hearing voices coming from the stairwell caught his attention. He glanced in to see the rear door open and people boarding from a small Zodiac boat. Jacob's muscles tightened, frozen in place, he scanned his surroundings for all threats, in front of him his worst nightmare.

Jacob observed the man from the wheelhouse barking out all the orders –

Vladimir. He was greeting the people boarding the ship. The first person that boarded he did not recognize, but the next two he knew all too well.

* * * *

Congressmen Norin and Congressmen Mitin were greeted with a handshake and a hug from Vladimir.

"Good to see you guys again, how long has it been," Vladimir said.

"Besides your phone calls recently about making big money, it has been about four years since our family reunion," Congressmen Norin said.

"Yeah, it's been four years," Mitin said.

"We have one problem Vladimir," Norin said.

"What's the problem"? Vladimir said.

"It's her," Norin said. A lady was pushed through the

door.

"Who the hell is she?" Vladimir said.

"She was helping me out on my campaign," Norin said. "We caught her prying into sensitive donor information. She walked out of my headquarters with the information about our partners; one of them was your dummy corporation information and name."

"Take the girl to my quarters, Dmitri; tie her up and lock her in," Vladimir said. "I will get to the bottom of what she's up to later."

"So where is all this profit you have for us?" Mitin said.

"Follow Dmitri through that hatch on the left, cousin, and I will show you our profits," Vladimir said. "Let's go through the engine room it is faster."

* * * *

Jacob's anger flooded his soul. His head pounded, as both fists clenched tight; he had to get a grip. He was in shock seeing Kate with those two crooked congressmen. He left the hatch ajar and walked to the other side of the walk. There was no choice; he opened the hatch and slipped in before being seen. Vladimir passed by with his group on to the catwalk and down toward the engine room.

Things had become deeply personal for Jacob. If Kate were to get hurt, he would never forgive himself. He knew her fate and this evil groups fate, were in his hands.

Jacob slid down to the bottom of the death room becoming soaked in blood and slime, he came to an abrupt stop, coming face to face with it, a large eye staring at him. No life in it. He turned away and another lifeless head stared at him. There must have been twenty whales' heads in the passageway leading all the way down to the rear door at the stern. The stench almost made Jacob lose his lunch he never had.

Damn, the devil is working overtime today. God willing, Kate and I will get through this.

What he did lose somewhere in the room was the AK-74 he was holding. It was gone, lost in the dark, cold, bloody, slimy death room. He had to retrieve another one. Things were not going as he had planned, seeing Kate captive made him wonder if this nightmare would ever end.

Jacob waited until the men started up the engines. He casually strolled down the stairs with his hat covering as much of his face as possible. The men standing next to the engine gave him a quick glance and went back to work. *Thank God they didn't realize I was not one of them.*

Jacob walked up to the men and shoved his AK-74 into the side of one of the man's head. They both froze, their eyes widened.

"Do not move or I will blow you both to hell. Get over to the work bench."

Jacob found zip ties and rope on the work bench. He used the zip ties and rope to secure their hands behind their backs and stuffed their mouths with greasy rags. "You criminals are going to hell, so get used to your new home." He pushed both men into the death room and closed the hatch.

Chapter 31

Vladimir showed his two partners all the meat cut up and neatly stacked in the refrigerated room on pallets covered in ice ready for shipment. His cousins were pleased. They would be able to fund their campaigns for years after they sold all this meat.

"Are you guys happy now?" Vladimir said.

"Yes, no doubts now," Mitin said.

"We will call our captain and have him bring our ship closer for transport," Norin said.

"Good, have him pull to the starboard side and we will start the transfer. Dmitri, get the men topside and prepare for the transfer. Now I go see what this woman knows."

"We will head back to our ship," Norin said. "I will let you know when the sale is complete, we should have the money in my account in a couple of days, I will transfer your share as soon as I get the money."

"That is what we are all here for," Vladimir said. "We will talk after our trip to the Arctic Circle, and it should be the biggest payday to date."

* * * *

Dmitri's voice was loud and clear all over the ship, as he ordered all the men to the wheelhouse. Some of the men showed up others did not.

"Where are the rest of the men? Dmitri asked.

The men raised their hands out to the side, shaking

their heads. Again, Dmitri ordered the men to the wheelhouse. No other men showed up.

"Go find them and tell them if they don't come to the wheelhouse their money may not show either," Dmitri said.

The men returned twenty minutes later.

"We searched the whole ship and we did not find them, we did find one big problem," A crewmen said.

"What," Dmitri said.

"One of our lifeboats is gone," he said.

"Gone, what do you mean gone."

"It's gone; the ropes were cut and spread out on the deck."

"I got to tell Vladimir; you men go get ready for the meat transfer I will be back."

* * * *

Vladimir sat down next to Kate and slapped her in the side of her face. "What in the hell are you doing lady," Vladimir whispered in her ear.

"I was just doing my job, I wasn't stealing anything, I was just bringing some work home with me," Kate said.

"I don't believe a word of it." Vladimir plugged a cord into a power outlet, set a bucket of water in front of Kate, and pulled off her shoes and socks. "Do you know what's going to happen next?"

He slapped Kate in the face with the back of his hand. Blood poured from her nose and mouth.

Kate said nothing, just stared defiant, at her captor.

"Have it your way, lady."

Vladimir held the wire over the bucket, and she

screamed in fear.

"Tell me the truth now or your dead body will be shark bait," Vladimir said.

"Ok," Kate mumbled. She'd had enough. "I will tell you what you want to know."

Kate talked. She confirmed what Norin told him about Jacob, her boyfriend. She mentioned he was trying to find out who killed all these dolphins that washed up on a beach in Oregon.

"What about the paperwork you were trying to steal?"

"He wanted me to find out who the big donors were, his company was losing all its funding, and he was hoping to find donors to keep them in business," Kate said.

"Ok, now that wasn't so hard, was it?"

Dmitri walked into Vladimir's quarters unplugged the cord.

"What do you want, Dmitri?"

"What are you doing man, she doesn't deserve this!" Dmitri said.

"It was quick and easy, and I got the information I wanted," Vladimir said.

"What happens to her now?

"Don't worry about her, I will take care of her. Are the men ready for the transfer?

"That's why I am here, we have a problem, six men and a life boat are missing," Dmitri said.

"What the hell, let's go, I'll find out what's going on."

"What about her," Dmitri said.

"She is not going anywhere," Vladimir said. "Let's get top side."

* * * *

Vladimir shook his head; He picked up the frayed rope laying on deck and slammed it on the railing. "We don't need this right now. This makes no sense, the men would not just leave, there is a big payday ahead for them."

"We searched everywhere for them they are not on board," Dmitri said.

"Well, search again! Scan the water for the raft, don't come back to the wheelhouse until you find them!"

"Ok boss," Dmitri replied.

Vladimir noticed his partner's ship pull to the starboard. He left the wheelhouse to help tie off the ship to the rust bucket for the transfer.

Dmitri called the men together on deck. "We need to search the ship again, Vladimir does not believe the men are gone; we need to search every inch of this ship."

Dmitri assigned each man a specific part of the ship to search. He personally went to a location no one probably searched – the stern, making his way through the engine room and up the stairs. He covered his nose and opened the hatch.

Dmitri peered into the dark room. "Anybody in here?" he yelled. A muffled groan from the back wall of the stern. Dmitri stepped into the chum room and called out again. Another muffled groan. He crawled over all the rotting whale heads down to the bottom.

He was covered in slime but found what he was searching for. There at the bottom by the door were two of the crewmen tied up and gagged. Dmitri untied the slime infective rope and freed them.

"What the hell happened to the two of you?"

"We were ambushed."

"Ambushed! What do you mean ambushed?"

"After servicing the engine, a guy came up on us out of nowhere; he had an AK pointed at my head and forced us up the stairs where he tied us up and threw us in here.

"Where are the others?" Dmitri said.

"No clue, it's just me and Igor."

Dmitri and the men crawled their way out of the death room covered in slime and ran back to the wheelhouse. Vladimir turned away, covered his nose.

"Are you clowns having fun, what in the hell are you idiots doing?"

"We have an intruder on board; he tied them up and forced them in the chum room," Dmitri said.

Vladimir's grin disappeared. "Dmitri have all the men armed and start searching for him."

"I guess we did not get rid of that lawman after all," Vladimir said. "Try not to kill him, I want to know who this fool is."

* * * *

Jacob made his way through the engine room into the main body of the ship. The factory ship was a monster, some 250-feet long and 70 feet wide.

Jacob Owens Brittles was hoping he wasn't lied to about the number of men aboard. He had taken down half the crew without much trouble and his confidence grew with each win. But this battle was nowhere near over. Kate was a prisoner and Vladimir was still killing.

He walked down the narrow hallway and stopped at

the first door, with ear to door, Jacob listened for a voice or any sound. There was none. He glanced in and seen two empty beds cramped into the small room. He entered the hallway and opened the next door, another empty room with two beds.

Jacob opened every door in the hallway and found nothing. He made his way down to the end of the hall and opened the last door. It opened up into the belly of the ship. There were stacks of whale meat on ice, the room was freezing. The roof to the deck was opened and men were hoisting pallets of meat top side.

Jacob skirted the port side wall behind the pallets of meat to the far side of the ships hold. He reached for the door knob, a shout echoed throughout the hold, "Search every room, search every inch of the ship, he is here somewhere!"

Jacob's jaw clenched tight. His time had run out. There would be no more surprises, they were on to him.

"Damn, I have to get to Kate fast and get her off this ship."

Jacob retreated back behind the pallets of meat; he squeezed between two stacks and pulled himself to the top of a pallet. They were near. Someone barked out orders..." search every inch, he is on the boat somewhere." They searched in front and behind every pallet. He pulled the clip to his AK to make sure he was ready if needed and a cold chill fell over his body, he realized, one bullet left. He could not believe it, *God why me? Why am I so stupid.*

He laid there shivering, buried in the meat, unable to

move in the freezing room. "Go check in there," a voice said. The five-foot slab blubber covering him, shook from someone pushing and poking at it. Jacob readied for the worst.

"Keep going, nothing here," a crewman said.

Jacob wiped slime from his face and aggressively tossed the slab off. He scanned around the room; the men had moved on.

Jacob had a dilemma, go back for a loaded AK in the stairway or find Kate without it. His choice was easy. He had to find Kate before Vladimir got to her. Jacob started toward the wheelhouse looking to find the living quarters and the captain's quarters near the wheelhouse. He came upon two doors, a tall roll up door with the chain on the side to raise and lower it. The other was unlocked and Jacob went through it. A rush of blistering heat pounded him in the face. He entered the noisy boiler room and sweat pooled on his forehead.

The steam from the boilers was everywhere, leaking out of every pipe on the ship. The pipes created a giant maze weaving in and out, going in every direction in the ship. It was a good break for Jacob. The steam would provide cover as he made his way forward, hoping to get closer to the helm, through this steam filled maze of metal. With the poachers searching for him, Jacob had to follow the path which took him deeper into the maze of piping and off the main corridor. He wiped the sweat from his face and continued forward ducking under and jumping over the hot piping.

The maze of metal was blistering hot. The pipes and

steam never stopped. He ducked under and jumped over piping, burning himself multiple times as he worked to escape this hell. He was getting angry; he wanted to scream out, but instead he punched through the cloud of steam in frustration.

Jacob knelt on the deck, looking under the floating hot steam. His face burned, he wanted over, he had no choice, giving up was not an option. Kate's life was in his hands.

Weaving in and out, over and under piping, finally the curtain of steam disappeared in front of him, he saw what he was hoping for, another door. *Thank God!*

Jacob turned the knob; it was unlocked. He hesitated for a second listening and then went through. This is the area of the ship Jacob was looking for. The corridor was short with doors on each side. *This has to be the sleeping quarters and galley area.*

Jacob checked inside every room down the hall, except the two at the end of the corridor and found nothing. He looked into the last one at the end of the hall and found the galley. He searched for a weapon of any kind. He found a knife; barely more intimidating than his pocket knife. He had one bullet in his pistol and a steak knife. Not much to take down these killers, but it is something. Kate was close, he had to get to her before Vladimir had his way with her. Jacob left the galley and stood in front of the last door and listened.

Chapter 32

Xian, Han and the rest of the crew of the *Sea Storm* – a 95-foot retired Coast Guard cutter made it to the beach in Oregon where Jacob wanted Xian to meet him.

"Well Han, he is not here, and he is not answering any phone or radio, what do you think?" Xian said.

"I can see the dead dolphins he was talking about on the beach, but he is nowhere in sight, maybe he found something; he would have contacted us and given a location if he was ok. We need to search the area."

"He could be anywhere, we start by going southwest and circle back north," Xian said.

"We did not see the boat at the dock on our way down here, he has to be somewhere out here," Han said.

Xian had the captain head southwest to start the search. They sailed for an hour southwest seeing nothing except for a few whales breaching the water heading north to the rich feeding grounds.

"We have seen nothing down here, we need to start heading north, while skirting the coast," Han said.

The captain turned the *Sea Storm* north following the path of the whales. The wind had picked up and the swells were growing.

"It is going to be a slow ride north," the captain said.

"We can't stop searching," Xian said.

The fog had dissipated and visibility kept improving as they reached the central Oregon coast line. Both Han and

Xian did not leave the helm; they were monitoring the sea with their high-powered binoculars. Both yelled out at the same time. "There is a boat."

"You see anyone on board?" Han said.

"No, but if you scan to the right, you will see a second boat."

"Two boats so close together – that can't be a coincidence."

"I do not see anyone in the other boat."

"The second boat has a cover on it for some reason," Han said.

"Get over there quick, Captain," Xian said.

The captain steered the *Sea Storm* toward the two boats floating a couple miles away. The closer they got the more they recognized, this might be the boat Jacob was using.

"That boat looks familiar," Han said.

"Jacob said he was using the same boat from back in the day," Xian said.

"Same color, same railing, same everything," Han said.

They pulled along the starboard side of the cruiser, they did not see anyone.

Han called out, "Is anyone there?"

There was no response.

Again, she yelled, "Is anyone there?"

Han went to the rear of the *Sea Storm* where the railing was the lowest and jumped over into the Cruiser. She searched below deck and found no one. As she continued to search, she noticed light coming through into the cabin. She investigated closer and noticed multiple holes with light coming through.

"Damn, the port side is full of what looks like bullet holes," Han yelled.

"See any blood?" Xian replied.

"No blood, keys still in the ignition in the on position."

Han turned the key, and the engine turned over.

Xian had stepped into the Cruiser. "It's not taking on water, everything looks ok."

"What do you mean everything looks ok, Xian? Jacob is not here! Everything is not ok!" Han yelled.

"I just meant the boat looks seaworthy," Xian said.

Xian ordered the captain to follow them on the cruiser to the second boat a short distance away. Xian pushed the throttle forward, and the cruiser plowed through the white caps. Within minutes they stopped next to the second boat.

"It is an old lifeboat, I'm not even sure they use old lifeboats like that anymore," Xian said.

"Get closer, I will remove the cover," Han demanded.

Han stepped back.

"What's wrong?" Xian yelled.

"Four men all tied up," Han said.

"I will inform the captain and have him pull closer so he can take them aboard," Xian said.

"I will untie them," Han said.

"Be careful Han," Xian said.

Han jumped over to the life boat and removed the gag from one of the men; he was dressed in camouflage pants and hat with a heavy jacket.

"What happened to you men?"

"Our ship was hijacked and they sent us away on this life boat,"

Han turned to Xian, standing on the bow. "They were hijacked."

"Hijacked, what does he mean hijacked?" Xian said.

Han untied the man's hands and told him to go aboard the cruiser and explain to Xian what happened. She continued to untie each of the men while Xian questioned the man. They all boarded the cruiser and were transported to the *Sea Storm*. Once the men were on board, Xian and Han tied the cruiser and life boat off to the *Sea Storm* and boarded.

"Captain start heading north, Jacob is in trouble," Xian said.

The four men were cold and hungry; Han showed them to the galley and left them there while she went to talk to Xian.

"Xian, what did the man have to say about what happened?" Han said

"He said they were fishing off the coast and a large boat pulled up next to them, fired off a few rounds in the air, and then stole all their fish and everything they had and sent them adrift on that old life boat."

"That is a big story, you believe?" Han said.

"It is weird, but with Jacob's boat so close to them maybe he was kidnapped by the same people that did this to them."

"Why would they not have put Jacob with them, and what's that accent they have, it's not American?" Han replied.

"I don't know, it's all speculation at this point, Han. We're heading the *Sea Storm* north, maybe we'll find some answers."

"I'm going to go check on the hostages and ask more questions," Han said.

"I'll go too," Xian said.

Xian and Han relieved the guard at the door to the galley. They heard chatter before they entered. Xian opened the door to complete silence. Before Xian said a word, two of the men brutally pounded on him. Han was thrown across the room into the sink, as she joined the fight. She fell to the deck in excruciating pain. Both laid on the floor battered and in complete shock. The men without hesitation duct taped their hands and mouths tight and wrapped their legs and arms together like a pair of mummies.

The Russians had taken over the unsuspecting crew of the *Sea Storm*. The crew of the Sea Storm were no match for these seasoned military men. All crewmen were duct taped and imprisoned in the galley alongside Xian and Han.

"Time to get back to the rust bucket and take our revenge on that lawman," the Russian said.

The Russian's had the *Sea Storm* heading north as fast as the sea would allow. The four split-up, one man guarded the prisoners, another searched the ship and the other two in the helm, one steering the ship the other tried, without success to contact Vladimir on the ships radio.

"We will catch up to them," the angry Russian said.

Chapter 33

Jacob pushed open the door into another large room that had two doors on either side. *This ship is just one endless set of doors, pipes and hallways, good for hiding but not so good for finding someone.* He opened a door and found a stairway leading topside and again another door on his right. He took the stairway, cautiously putting pressure on each creaking wooden step. His pistol with one round was no match for these hunter killer criminals. He stopped on the last step; A loud crack sound. *Man, bad luck that last step.* Jacob dove into the room expecting a shootout, but no one was in the helm. He peeked out the windows and noticed men offloading the whale meat on to another ship. He had no doubt it was the congressmen's ship. He saw Vladimir barking out orders to the men offloading their catch. Jacob considered using his one bullet to take out Vladimir, he was within range. The risk of missing was too big. The background noise from the radio kept calling to Jacob's attention. He focused in on what was being said, and his heart started to pound a little faster.

"Vladimir, this is Victor, come in. Vladimir, this is Victor, come in. If you can hear me, come in! We were set adrift on the lifeboat by that lawman. We were rescued by an environmental group; we have taken over their ship. We are on our way back to you, so don't shoot us."

* * * *

Jacob sent out a couple of distress calls on the radio with no response, hoping Vladimir's men were not monitoring the call. He cut the wire supplying power to the radio and headed down the stairs to the last door left to check, and there she was.

Kate was on the floor, tied to the bed rail. She jerked her head back.

"Am I dreaming?"

"No, you're not dreaming."

"How did you get here? Kate said.

"It is a long story, and we don't have the time to talk about it right now, we need to get off this ship."

"Congressman Norin found me taking information out of his headquarters and kidnapped me; they brought me here on a cargo ship."

"I saw Norin and Congressman Mitin come aboard with you. It looks like they're in on this poaching operation of the Russian poacher Vladimir; they're offloading tons of whale meat on that cargo ship as we speak."

"How are we going to escape?" Kate mumbled.

"If we can get to the rear of the ship, we might be able to take one of the two boats tied off at the stern."

"What boat brought you here.?"

"Our old reliable."

"Thank God."

"We will take whatever boat we can to get you off this ship to safety; let's go, the crewmen are already searching for me, we don't have a lot of time."

Jacob and Kate made it unseen past the steam and hot pipes of the boiler room into the cold storage where the whale meat was. Most of the meat was gone having already been transferred to the cargo ship of the Congressmen. The bearded crewman was hooking up the last of the pallets as Kate and Jacob slipped by him and made it into the long hallway.

They were halfway down the hall, close to the engine room and the AK-74 Jacob hid under the stairs. The patter of footsteps alerted them. They ducked into the first unlocked door just as the men entered the hall.

"Check every room, they have to be down here somewhere," Dmitri said. Jacob and Kate had nowhere to go; they were trapped in a small room. The voices got louder and louder as another door closed. Room after room they searched.

Jacob and Kate sat on the bunk and accepted their fate. They heard them tearing apart the room next to them. Jacob got up and locked the door as the only meaningless thing left to do and sat with pistol in hand and one bullet left. They stared at the door knob, as it turned back and forth. They were expecting it to be kicked in, a screeching shout over the loudspeaker, suddenly the knob stopped turning... "Everyone get top side now, we have a large ship approaching and it does not look like a friendly fishing vessel. Dmitri get the men top side and armed!"

Jacob and Kate turned toward each other; their eyes opened wide. They couldn't believe their good fortune. The commotion stopped, the men searching were gone, the hallway was clear. Jacob and Kate hurried into the engine room and up the stairs onto the cat walk.

Jacob opened the door to the starboard side stairway

and found his AK-74 right where he hid it. He checked the magazine and found it had two rounds, not enough to make a stand, but it was better than nothing.

"Stay close, Kate. Are you strong enough to swim to one of the boats tied to the stern if we need to?"

"Yes, I can do it."

Jacob opened the door at the stern of the factory ship. A sinking feeling in his stomach hit hard, nothing was there, not even the fishing boat Jacob was expecting.

"Our good luck didn't last long," Jacob said.

"Look over there, that ship, it's coming right for us," Kate said.

"It is the *Sea Storm*, the ship Xian brought down from Seattle."

"Maybe we will have a future," Kate said.

The *Sea Storm* nestled close to the port side on the rust bucket, Jacob recognized the person on the bow.

"That is one of the prisoners I set adrift on a life boat before you arrived, Xian must have found them," Jacob said.

"Why is the Russian standing on the bow waving?" Kate said.

"Xian and crew were hijacked. Poachers have taken over the ship somehow!"

"What now?"

"Take this AK-74 and stay here, I need to get on the *Sea Storm* and find out what has happened to Xian and Han," Jacob said.

Jacob watched as the *Sea Storm* pulled alongside and tied off. Kate stood next to him. She gave him a nod, holding up the AK-74 in one hand and waved at him to go forward with the other.

Jacob shuffled topside; under the cover of darkness, he headed for one of the docking lines holding the two ships together. Kate was anxious and moved to the door and watched Jacob slide hand over fist on the dock line to the *Sea Storm*. Within minutes Jacob had boarded the *Sea Storm* and disappeared from sight.

Kate turned to go back down the stairs and found herself looking down the barrel of 9mm pistol.

"Give me that gun," the man demanded.

Kate dropped the gun and was pushed to the ground and stepped on, holding her down.

"Bring her to Vladimir in the wheelhouse; I have the fishing boat coming around to pick me up so I can transfer the prisoners from our captured ship and another moneymaker," Dmitri said.

Chapter 34

Jacob headed below deck. He readied himself for a fight. He entered the hallway. There was complete silence. He had to get to the helm. Jacob took the least likely corridor to the helm bypassing the kitchen and crew's quarters. He moved down the corridor, and at the stairs to the helm he heard something coming from the communications room. He eased the door open a sliver and peeked through, then slammed the door open, 9mm in hand. A crewman was searching the room.

"What are you looking for?" Jacob said.

The man turned, raised a gun and fired but rushed his shot and missed. Jacob returned fire from his pistol, and the man buckled with a shot to the stomach. Jacob recognized the Russian poacher from the lifeboat he set adrift. He retrieved the poacher's gun and turned his attention to the corridor where footsteps pounded the floor and yelling echoed throughout the narrow hallway.

Jacob hid behind the door, as the man rushed into the comm room.

The man knelt next to his shipmate. "What happened, where is all this blood coming from?"

Before he answered, Jacob had his gun pushed up against the man's head.

"You again, don't you ever stop?" the Russian said.

"You guys had your chance to go quietly; you chose to take over one of my ships, and now one of your friends is dying."

"I meant what I said back on the factory ship – Vladimir is out of control, he killed a friend of mine, and if you want my help, I will help you," Pavel said.

Jacob stared the Russian down, scratched his head, considering what he'd said.

"You will be the first to go down if you cross me," Jacob said.

Commotion in the corridor caught his attention, he wasn't ready for a shootout until he found Han, Xian and the crew.

"I'm going to have a gun on you at all times, so tell them everything is ok in here, you are just checking on the communications equipment," Jacob said.

"Ok," Pavel said.

Dmitri pounded on the door to the comm room. "Pavel, where are the prisoners?" Dmitri said.

"They are down the hall, Dmitri, why?" Pavel said.

"Don't worry about it, make sure this ship is ready to sail; you will have to pilot this ship by yourself."

Pavel was true to his word, he told Dmitri what he wanted to hear, he never stopped, although most people with a gun to their head would do the same. Jacob, still leery of his Russian prisoner, pulled him back into the room.

"Look, your shipmate is dead, this could have been avoided if..." Jacob stopped abruptly in mid-sentence. "We need to get to the bridge, get moving Pavel."

Jacob and Pavel took the long way around to the bridge, hoping to avoid any of the poachers. They were surprised to find the bridge empty. Jacob scanned the deck and didn't see anyone. He did see them transfer Xian, Han and crew to the fishing boat and removed the docking lines.

"Pavel, sit on the floor and do not move or I will blow your head off. Jacob started up the engines and slowly backed away from the port side of the factory ship to its stern to pick up Kate. She was not where she was supposed to be. Panic and anger hit Jacob. She was nowhere to be seen. What he did see angered him even more. At the stern where Kate should have been was Dmitri offloading Xian, Han from the fishing boat.

Jacob backed the *Sea Storm* away from the factory ship. It did not go unnoticed by Vladimir sitting at the helm of the factory ship. Vladimir could see into the illuminated bridge of the *Sea Storm* and realized right away it wasn't one of his men piloting the ship.

Both men sat in their wheelhouse staring at each other. As Jacob backed the *Sea Storm* away from the factory ship, a voice over the ship's load speaker invaded the helm. Hearing the heavy Russian accent, that son of a bitch, Vladimir.

"You have been a pain in the ass for far too long," Vladimir said.

"And you have been breaking the law for far too long!" Jacob yelled.

"You need to bring back my new ship, and I will let you and your crew members go in peace," Vladimir said.

"I can't do it. This is not my ship to give away."

"Well, it's the ship or..." Vladimir paused, a look of disbelief crushed his face. "...what the hell? You two look all too familiar. I'll deal with you later, lawman."

Han and Xian were pushed into the wheelhouse, and Vladimir stepped inches from Xian face.

"You two work for that lawman, is that what's going on? You two have been setting me up, or should I say trying to set me up for a long time," Vladimir said.

"We work for AECEN, and yes, we have been after you and all your murderous crew," Xian said. "We finally have you; before long, there will be three naval ships here to take you down."

"I guess I should just give up," Vladimir said.

"It will go easier on you if you do," Han said.

"You played your part really good lady; you had me fooled in that bar back in Vietnam," Vladimir said.

"It does not matter now, your time is at an end," Han replied.

"I would not be so confident; it will never be over until I say it's over," Vladimir yelled.

"Vladimir!" Jacob yelled over a bull horn.

"I hear you, lawman!" Vladimir screamed into the ship's speaker.

"It's over, give it up," Jacob said.

"Get all of them on deck, Dmitri; put them on the bow where the lawman can see them!" Vladimir screamed.

"Vladimir, you have nowhere to go – it's over, give up," Jacob demanded.

"I want you to focus on the bow of my ship in the next couple of minutes and then you will have my answer lawman," Vladimir replied.

Jacob and Pavel stared at the bow of the factory ship from the bridge, waiting for Vladimir's next move.

"What do you think he has in mind, Pavel?" Jacob said.

"Whatever it is, it can't be good," Pavel said.

Jacob had his answer. Kate, Xian and Han and crew were all marched to the bow of the factory ship. Their hands tied. They were pushed up against the rail on the starboard side of bow facing Jacob in the *Sea Storm*.

"Do you see your friends on the bow lawman?" Vladimir said.

"Yeah, I see them, what do you have in mind, a trade? If you hurt them in any way, there will be nowhere to hide."

"You will see," Vladimir said, as he walked out on to the deck and stood in front of Jacob's three best friends and crewmen. Vladimir stood in front of the crew of the *Sea Storm* and shot all the men in the head and had them tossed overboard. He shuffled over to Han, stared into her eyes, shoved a pistol to the side of her head and fired.

Han crumbled to the deck and laid there lifeless, blood pouring from the side her head. Xian went into a rage and charged Vladimir and knocked him to the ground, head butting him before Vladimir's men pulled him off and restrained him. Xian did not stop struggling. He kept fighting with the men holding him until one of them hit him in the head with a butt of a pistol. He fell next to Han's motionless body. Xian stared in disbelief, as tears rolled down his face. The love of his life was gone.

Vladimir picked up Han's body and tossed it overboard like a worthless piece of whale meat. Shocked and raging, Xian fought to get up, but Dmitri had his foot on his neck holding him down. Kate stood there in complete disbelief, tears running down her face, knowing she was next. She fell to her knees and prayed.

"Get up off your knees and stop praying to a false God, woman; stand them both up and have them face the lawman again," Vladimir screamed.

Vladimir pointed at Jacob in defiance all the way to the wheelhouse, in the helm he mocked Jacob on the ship's loud speaker.

"You think I would surrender to a clown like you?" Vladimir shouted. "You incompetent idiots have been trying to defeat me for years and haven't done it yet, what makes you believe you can stop me now?"

"There is no place on earth you will be able to hide. You will pay with everything you have and everything you cherish in this world for this, that I will promise you."

"You are an incompetent fool if you believe that. Now watch as another one of your friends becomes shark bait."

Vladimir put his hand up to his head like a gun and pulled the trigger giving Dmitri the order to shoot the next one. Dmitri raised his pistol to the head of Xian; he jerked his head back and charged toward Kate and leaped with all his force at her. Both tumbled over the railing. Dmitri and his men were stunned, and hesitated for a second looking at each other.

"Kill them!" Vladimir said.

The men started firing into the water at Kate and Xian. Both surfaced for air and quickly dove as bullets splashed around them.

They fired until they were all out of ammo, minutes went by, they didn't see either resurface. Vladimir pushed through his men to the railing.

"Did they cone up yet Dmitri?" Vladimir said.

"No, it's been a couple of minutes, nothing," Dmitri said.

Vladimir hurried back to the helm, for the load speaker. Before he could mock the lawman, he spotted the Sea Storm moving. Something he wasn't expecting, from this incompetent lawman.

"Pavel go cut loose the boats in tow and hurry back," Jacob said. Jacob put the *Sea Storm* into gear and headed for the factory ship.

"Pavel, I need you to be true to your word, will you help me," Jacob said.

"Yes, I want nothing to do with that murderer," Pavel said.

"Pavel, are you ready to make things right?"

"Yeah, I'm ready."

"Take over the wheel and head right for them, we will take them down one way or the other," Jacob said.

Jacob stepped aside as Pavel took the wheel and he ran for the bow of the *Sea Storm*. He engaged the machine gun and fired at the massive factory ship firing until he had nothing left and masterfully reloaded and continued to fire until the factory ship had stalled in its attempt to escape. Jacob reloaded again and fired hundreds of rounds that pounded the factory ship.

The poachers were ducking for cover, the ones able.

The factory ship was quickly disabled. The poachers were strewn all over the deck. He waved Pavel to keep going. Smoke filled the air, heat radiated off the machine gun, his ears pained. Jacob didn't stop; he unloaded every bullet he had left into the helm and stern of the factory ship.

The *Sea Storm* reached full speed and rammed into the side of the factory ship. The violent collision stopped both ships dead. The factory ship rolled to one side as the *Sea Storm* broke through the rusted hull, bending and crushing metal, as it came to a stop. Debris scattered every direction, smoke billowed up from below. Jacob's chest slammed into the machine gun so hard, the bolts holding the machine gun in place snapped, propelling him into the railing on the bow. Jacob held on to the machine gun as it hung over the weakened railing, gasping for air. The weight became too much, breaking the railing and sending both the machine gun and Jacob into the Pacific as the *Sea Storm* floated back out from the belly of the beast.

Jacob's chest pained as he swam past the gaping hole in the side of the factory ship toward the bow, as it started to list to its port side. He searched for Kate and Xian to see if they were still alive and found an empty ocean. He yelled for them, only silence. His soul pained.

Jacob did not want to believe he had lost his best friends at the hand of Vladimir. His only hope was they started to swim toward shore.

Jacob swam back to the *Sea Storm* at the end of his rope, a gut punch turned to fright seeing a hole the size of bucket in the starboard side, and the *Sea Storm* was taking in water fast. The *Sea Storm* started to sink lower and lower and was not long for the bottom of the Pacific. He yelled out to Pavel, "Abandon ship, abandon ship!"

There was no response.

Jacob had no choice. He swam away from the *Sea Storm,* as it disappeared from his sight. Behind the disappearing *Sea Storm,* he saw the giant factory ship burning and smoking. It did not look good; it would not be long before it joined the *Sea Storm.*

Jacob had one choice. He started for the beach two miles away; the current was in his favor. The fate of Kate and Xian invaded his soul. It would not leave his mind. Jacob prayed and rested, floating on his back. He hoped that he would see his friends safe on the beach waiting for him.

Jacob was close enough to see the outcropping of rocks he was quite familiar with, the same ones Han, Xian and himself would explore diving in and around back in college. Jacob rested; hell attacked his mind... he questioned himself... was there something different that he could have done to save his friends. The guilt was starting to get the best of him. His stomach churned, thinking he let Han, Kate and Xian down. *It's my fault they all might be dead. I don't think I'm worthy of such friends.*

* * * *

Vladimir fell to the deck and slid down into the water, as the ship began to turn over. He boarded the cruiser not far off and watched as the old rust bucket disappeared into the deep of the pacific.

A hole in the skyline appeared, as the massive rust bucket disappeared. Vladimir pounded on the steering wheel, screaming obscenities. Pushing the throttle forward, he turned toward port, his relatives and buyers of the meat would help him. He spotted to his surprise, two prisoners were floating not fifty yards away, both on their backs kicking away toward shore. They had no idea what was about to descend on them. Vladimir motored toward them; he stopped inches from them, creating a wake that washed over them.

"Where do you two think you're going?" Vladimir said. "I admire your resilience, trying to get to shore with your hands tied, but I am not done with you two yet."

Vladimir took the gaff with a hook on the end and hooked Xian on the leg, ripping into his pants and cutting his leg. Xian yelled every swear word in his vocabulary at Vladimir. A cloud of blood surrounded Xian. Vladimir pulled him into the boat by his hair and the back of his collar. He gaffed Kate in the pant leg and pulled her close, pulling her in by her collar. Blood trickled onto the deck, and a lifeless look dominated Kate's face. Vladimir tossed them to the bench seat and tied them up. He scanned the surface, looking for any crewmen who might have survived.

"Your lawman killed the both of you," Vladimir said. "I will find him and he will feel the pain of your deaths, before his own."

* * * *

Jacob stopped floating and started swimming toward the beach a few hundred yards away. He stopped and rested after each swell released him. While he rested, a familiar noise gave him hope, a motor boat. Jacob waited for the next swell to raise him upward. The boat was circling, getting closer to the beach with each pass. Jacob waved his arms back and forth in the air hoping to be seen. The boat turned toward Jacob. As it came into clear view, the more familiar the boat looked to Jacob. Jacob focused on the person driving. He became clear. Vladimir! Jacob looking through his salt infused burning eyes noticed the silhouette of two other people with Vladimir.

Chapter 35

Vladimir found the target he was searching for. He was a short distance away waving his hands in the air.

"I can't believe this dumbass lawman waving me over was the one who has destroyed my whole operation. He and you two are going to pay with your lives," Vladimir said. He pushed them both down into the galley.

Vladimir pushed the throttle forward and turned right for Jacob, as he floated bobbing up and down in the frigid water. Jacob quickly dove down to avoid Vladimir's attempt to run him over. He resurfaced as Vladimir turned around for a second pass. He dove down again as Vladimir passed by overhead. Vladimir made a quick turn around and was right on top of him, as he surfaced, barely giving Jacob time to dive down a couple feet to avoid the propeller.

Jacob was losing the cat and mouse battle; he was exhausted and having trouble holding his breath. Vladimir was relentless. Jacob had no choice he swam for the outcropping of rocks. As he surfaced for air, Vladimir headed right for him again. Jacob dove again just missing the propeller as Vladimir passed over him. Vladimir turned sharply and waited for Jacob to surface again. Jacob did not surface. Five minutes passed, Vladimir circled his boat by the outcropping of rocks and seen nothing. He knew he didn't hit him; *maybe he just drowned,* he thought. Vladimir had to see the body of the lawman.

He took a knife from the captain's drawer and jumped in. He dove down into the semi clear water and swam around the rocks ten feet below the surface. He re-surfaced, took a deep breath and dove again. His third dive he found a large underwater opening, into the rock formation.

* * * *

Jacob rested on the rock shelf catching his breath, the calm surface water in the cave started to agitate. He searched for anything that might be used as a weapon and found nothing. He stood up ready for whatever fate might await him.

His head breached the surface. Only it was not Vladimir as Jacob was expecting but a seal. The seal did not seem afraid, even with Jacob standing there. It jumped out of the water and onto the rock Jacob was standing on. Jacob jumped back, the seal moved away from the water its head rotating left and right. Jacob sensed something was not right; he readied himself for the worst. It did not take long.

Vladimir exploded out of the water, breaching the surface gasping for air with knife protruding out in front of him. Jacob did not hesitate he jumped in right on top of Vladimir before he could get a full breath of air. He drove him to the bottom of the water. Vladimir swung the knife at Jacob, slicing his forearm. Jacob landed a few blows to Vladimir's stomach. He lost what air he had left and kicked toward the surface. Jacob followed and latched on to his leg and attempted to pull him down to the bottom. Vladimir kicked at Jacob's hands with everything he had. Jacob's strength was waning; he could not hold on any longer.

Vladimir escaped to the surface, sucking in air like a fish out of water. Jacob swam deeper into the cave to the next opening thirty yards away. He was familiar with cave like no other. His father and his friends explored almost every inch of it back in college. Jacob swam to a dry sandy area and waited for what would come next, he became enraged thinking about what Vladimir had just taken from him. All his friends were dead, his future wife dead, his future gone.

Jacob hoped Vladimir would follow after him, he wanted to end this here and now, the place where he and his friends had spent so many great days exploring the underwater caves. Jacob was aware of the areas of darkness and the area that were illuminated by an opening at the top.

God, help me stop this madman here and now.

Jacob waited on the sand hoping he would show up. Ten minutes passed; Vladimir did not show.

"What is this killer doing now? Is he waiting me out in the other section of the cave or did he leave like the coward he is before I could capture or kill him.

Jacob had to move, staying there was no longer an option; he had to go after this murderer now!

Ripping off a sleeve from his blood-soaked shirt, he rang it out and covered the gash on his arm to slow the bleeding. The more Jacob thought about Vladimir escaping again, it drained his soul, he had to go on the offensive, even without a weapon.

Jacob placed a foot back into the water, and readied to dive in, the calm water in the cave started to rise. The water rose like a powerful wave crashing into shore. Jacob backed away from the water's edge expecting Vladimir to swim in, with help.

There was no Vladimir, what Jacob saw was worse than ten Vladimir's. It was a giant dorsal fin, too big to be a dolphin. One of his biggest fears had just joined him in the underwater cave.

The shark swam around the edges of the cave, as if circling its prey. "This is crazy," He was trapped, and Vladimir had to be long gone. Jacob's arm pounded, then his head joined in. He kicked sand toward the fin and let out a scream in anguish. He had to accept the fact that Vladimir would escape again.

God, why is this happening?

The twelve-foot Great White circled for ten minutes, occasionally popping its massive head out of the water to stare at Jacob standing a couple feet away. Its head would submerge out of sight leaving the large dorsal patrolling the cave. Jacob waited, watching the calm water for any slight movement, any small ripple expecting it to resurface.

Jacob waited and watched, never taking his eyes away from the surface. Fixated on the calm surface of the water, he thought about leaving the cave to go after Vladimir. He wanted to get him in the worst way but his biggest fear had just been feet away. The great white imprisoned him in this cold dark place.

A half hour went by without seeing any sign of the monster. Jacob clapped his hands, trying to force in confidence. He stood closer to the water's edge, conflicted, every time he decided to leave, he stopped and questioned whether the shark was lurking below the surface waiting for a meal. Jacob sat down at the edge of the sand bar and kept his sight on the surface. His eyes strained from staring so intently at the water. He closed his eyes for a brief second to refocus.

Jacob opened his eyes and found the monster was staring at him just feet away, its head resting partially on the edge of the sand bar. Jacob's face heated, and in a panic, he pushed into the sand with his feet and hands, backing away from the water's edge to the cave wall. The shark was there for a couple of seconds and then slipped off the sand and back into the water and disappeared. Jacob spotted something, in the kicked-up sand, a shiny object protruding; he pulled it out and shook loose a chain from the compacted sand. A second chain with a pendent attached to the first, came with it. Connected to the rusted chain were two dog tags. Jacob rubbed off the crusted sand and dirt. Most of the information was readable. The first three letters Jac were clear, next to them Brittles. Jacob opened the pendent to see a picture still intact, his mother's smiling face appeared. Tears puddled and flowed down Jacob's face, his head down, jaw clenched tight. The dog tags Jacob had made for himself while in the Guard, the same ones he sent to his dad a year before he left the Coast Guard and the missing pendent that dad left hanging in the helm of his boat.

"Rest in peace, love yah both."

Jacob shook loose from his sadness by the weird behavior from the shark. He didn't understand it until he saw them. There were three small fins protruding above the surface of the water swimming toward the sandy area. All three baby Great Whites stopped and swam back and forth near the sandy area of the underwater cave.

Jacob was shocked and amazed, one of his greatest fears probably gave birth to its offspring in the cave. It gave him a different prospective with his fear of the Great White. Still cautious, he stayed a distance away not wanting to get to close to the water. Jacob had a past with these sharks while diving here a couple years ago. The giant wasn't interested in him that day.

Jacob watched in amazement as the baby sharks swam back and forth for a few minutes and then as quickly as they appeared they were gone. Jacob continued to watch for any movement in the crystal-clear water of the cave. He moved to the edge of the sand bar, scanning for movement, none appeared, his thoughts returned to Vladimir and capturing him before he escaped.

He was inching his way back into the water when it sprung out on to the wet sand. Jacob fell backwards as it beached its head on the sand bar, its mouth wide open, the black eyes and its large sharp teeth closed to within inches of Jacob's foot as he lay on the sand. Jacob took a few deep breaths, his heart pounded, his brain stuck.

Jacob stared at the killer shark; seconds had passed and it slithered back into the water and disappeared.

Jacob sat there for twenty minutes, moving his head side to side and hands stretched out to his side – *Why do these things keep happening to me?*

Jacob's mind was tortured; he was there for too long trying to get up the nerve to reenter the water. There was no sign of the beast. Over twenty minutes past since he stared into the black eyes of the beast. Before Jacob went after Vladimir, he reminded himself not to lose his soul while taking down this killer. *Do it the right way. Semper Paratus.*

Jacob dove in head first and swam to the bottom figuring the shark would not be laying on the bottom waiting and it wasn't. The shark and the babies were nowhere to be seen. The light from the opening above gave him confidence as he pushed through the clear water. His visibility away from the sandy beach was thirty to forty feet. No giant fish in sight, maybe another test, a JOB test? He prepared himself.

Jacob swam to the surface for a breath and swam toward the entrance to the cave. Half way to the entrance he spotted him, swimming toward Jacob deeper into the cave. Vladimir! Jacob stopped and surfaced for air and climbed up onto a rock shelf exposed by the low tide and waited. Surprise was on his side.

Jacob could see Vladimir wasn't much of a swimmer, splashing around, making a lot of noise. Vladimir was close to the large opening toward the back of the cave. Jacob took a deep breath and dove down a few feet and swam underwater toward Vladimir. His legs kicking ten feet away. Jacob finally had the criminal right where he wanted him.

Jacob's mind was racing the closer he got to Vladimir. This man just stabbed him in the last encounter; he would not under estimate him again. Jacob would take him by surprise and hold nothing back. *It's going to be him or me.* Jacob let Vladimir swim deeper into the cave. This was playing right into Jacob's hands. He had an advantage knowing the caves. Vladimir did not. Jacob knew the deeper you get into this maze of underwater channels the darker it got. This was another advantage for Jacob. He kept following him into the darkest area of the caves and would take him there.

Jacob followed, one breaststroke at a time. Vladimir grunted and splashed like a child learning how to swim. Jacob had no doubt this killer was relentless and had to have his revenge. He would not stop until he killed Jacob. Vladimir kept searching, swimming deeper into the cave. They approached the darkest section and the farthest point Jacob had ever been. It was pitch black. The water and smell of the cave changed; the water had a frothy look to it and there was a strong musty, fish smell that was choking, Jacob had trouble breathing from the stench. His visibility just two feet. Vladimir was close, still splashing around like a dead fish.

Jacob's nightmare had to end here and now. He was closing in on him, ready to end this, until something from below nudges him. It was enough of a nudge to throw him off his rhythm. Jacob froze, moving just enough to keep afloat.

A chill covered the back of Jacob's neck, his breathing

quickened. Then another nudge, he swam to the wall of the cave and was nudged again. He clutched the cave wall and watched for a clue to what it might be.

Vladimir yelled out "What the hell are you! what are you?

He is feeling a JOB moment, Jacob mumbled.

Jacob knew the hell he was in. Shark fins protruding above the surface started to appear. Not just one but others passed by and circled. He heard Vladimir scream again and again as the sharks swam past him. There was something strange about the sharks, for they did not seem at all aggressive. They just swam by and disappeared somewhere into or out of the cave.

Jacob heard Vladimir swimming back in his direction mumbling something in Russian. He wanted to yell out to him to shut up and get against the wall but didn't. Jacob used the cave wall to pull himself back toward the entrance with as little movement as possible. Vladimir was beside himself, making a lot of noise. They didn't attack him, but with all the noise he was making eventually that will happen. Jacob did not want to be in the water if their aggressiveness started. He had no doubt that this was a birthing cave for the Great White. *This is not even their known migration area. It's unheard of for these sharks to even be this far north now. The temperature change in the Pacific might have something to do with it.*

Jacob pulled himself along the wall, eye to eye with some of the biggest sharks swimming just feet from him. He made it to the large cavernous opening with only an occasional tail swipe by one of the monsters. Their tail skin was rough, not smooth, like he once assumed.

Jacob heard rocks crashing into the water as Vladimir climbed the wall of the cave, his moaning slowed to an occasional grunt, as he wallowed out of the water. Jacob pulled himself along the wall, he seen an underwater opening. In all the years he, Xian and Han dove here, they never explored this four-foot-wide opening. It would be risky to enter the opening but if it led him away from the sharks and out of the cave it would be worth it. Vladimir was going nowhere. Vladimir would sit on these rocks until high tide forced him back into the water. If this opening led nowhere, Jacob would still have time to double back and catch Vladimir.

Jacob entered the four-foot-wide opening and noticed a faint light illuminating from the bottom of the cave about forty feet in and twenty feet down. It looked like a possible escape route. He swam into the opening just above the light, took a deep breath and dove down to the light source. Jacob's strength and swimming skills enabled him to make it down to the light source.

Jacob reached the light below, his head dropped, more gloom set in, he found six small holes no bigger than a bowling ball was letting the light through from outside of the cave. His lungs were running on empty, hope fading fast. He kicked and pushed to the surface, breaking through for much needed air. Discouraged and exhausted he was back in hell with the Sharks and the murderer Vladimir, *"is this nightmare ever going to end,"* he thought.

The giant sharks and their offspring were still moving in and out of the cave. Jacob kept close to the wall pulling himself toward the opening and freedom. That was not to be, Vladimir was in front of him clinging to the one rock ledge, left above water. The tide was rising and the rock and Vladimir would be underwater. Vladimir would have to leave the safety of the rock soon. Jacob waited, holding on the side of the cave. Jacob was sure Vladimir would stop at the safety of the sandy beach in the large cavern. This is where Jacob would end this crazy Russian.

The murderer held on until the tide rose and fully took away his safety. Fifteen feet away, Jacob seen Vladimir enter the shark infested water, moaning.

He noisily swam along the wall toward the sandy beach. Jacob stayed ten feet back, if he stopped Jacob would stop. Vladimir made the beach, laid on the sand like a dead seal, moaning. Jacob silently approached the beach submerged, his eyes and forehead above the water line. Vladimir laid there on his back, his chest rising and falling with each deep breath.

This was Jacob's clue to end it now. Jacob burst out of the water and took him by surprise. Jacob stomped on his arm, as he pulled the knife out. Without hesitation he kicked him in the head three times, like a mad man, he punched him in the rib's multiple times. Vladimir laid there dazed, Jacob picked up the knife and pushed it up to his chin.

"Your days of murder are over!" Jacob said.

"It's never going to be over for me," Vladimir said.

"Shut up you son of a bitch," Blood rushed into Jacob's

face, he kicked him in the ribs a few more times, after each kick he repeated, "This is for Kate, this is for Han, and this is for Xian."

Vladimir laid there moaning, bleeding from his mouth and nose. "I will get you for this!" he screamed.

"You are done, don't fight it. You murdered my friends; I will not hesitate to kill you."

Jacob took Vladimir's belt and wrapped it around his wrists and cinched it tight. He circled his belt around Vladimir's belt and cinched it. He finally had this murdering sociopath. Jacob took a deep breath, The tension in his muscles relaxed, his soul elated. The nightmare was finally over.

With Vladimir bleeding bad, there was no way they would be able to swim out of the cave. Jacob decided to scale the rocks to the small opening above. Jacob pulled him to his feet, he staggered, Jacob pushed him in the direction of the rock wall. The footing was slippery. Moss and algae covered the jagged rocks, an earthy and damp smell covered Jacob's clothes, the smell invaded every breath.

Jacob pushed Vladimir up toward the opening. Vladimir struggled with his hands tied, but they made it to the half-way point without too much trouble. The last twenty feet steepened. They stood on a rock halfway up and rested, Jacob made Vladimir stand on a rock facing the cave wall. He peered down toward the sandy beach, a couple of the giant sharks circled.

"You better listen to everything I say or you will end up down there," Jacob said.

"Jacob pulled Vladimir from the edge and pushed him up toward the light. Each step was meticulously taken. At the top, Jacob pulled on Vladimir's collar and stopped him. "I need to go out first and pull you through the opening, you won't be able to pull yourself out with your hands tied."

Jacob crawled around Vladimir on the steepest section of the cliff. He crawled past him and stepped toward the opening. Vladimir grasped Jacob's legs; he slid down the rocks a couple of feet before he gained control. His hands and knees scraping against the jagged rocks, cutting his hands, blood dripped down his wrists. Jacob screamed in pain. Vladimir held on tight.

"You son of a bitch! this not going to end well for you,"

Vladimir swung his other arm around Jacob's legs and violently twisted and turned back and forth trying to dislodge Jacob from his foothold. Jacob secured his foot hold and struck Vladimir in the head, punch after punch until he let go with one hand, one last kick with all he had. Vladimir let go. He started to slip down the rocks. Jacob grabbed the belt and stopped him from sliding out of reach, the pain in his hands burned. Vladimir was unable to gain a footing, his legs flailing wildly. Jacob's hold was tight but he was straining to keep it.

"Get a foothold; I can't hold you for much longer," Jacob said.

"I can't, it's too slippery, lawman."

Jacob had both feet firmly set on the rocks and reached down with his left hand. He was able to get a hand on to the belt. Vladimir stopped kicking and was just hanging over the water.

"Pull yourself up!" Jacob shouted. Sweat beaded off Jacob's forehead, dripping into Vladimir's face

Vladimir said nothing.

"I know what happened to your wife and kid back in Russia; it wasn't your fault they got trampled to death in the riot at the Ministry building." Jacob grunted.

Vladimir's eyes narrowed; a look of pure evil flushed his face. He put both feet against the rock wall and pushed, all his weight pulling on Jacob, Jacob's jaw tightened, his head jerked back against the rocks. Vladimir pulled down hard, trying to pull both of them off the rocks. The belt began to loosened. It started to unravel and slipped from Jacob's grasp.

Vladimir freed one hand out from the belt and latched onto Jacob's pant leg, he shook the pant leg violently, rocks began to fracture, a crackling startled Jacob. They crumbled under foot. Jacob lost footing with one leg. Vladimir grabbed for Jacob's other leg. Jacob had no choice, he let go of the belt. Vladimir outstretched hands had a hold on Jacob's pant leg. He attempted to pull him down, but could not. He tried to grasp the other leg, Jacob sat down for more leverage. He leaned back as far as possible on the cliff and planted blow after blow to Vladimir's head until his eyes rolled back into his head. Dazed, broken and bloody. He lost his grip.

Vladimir fell ten feet and bounced off a rock and fell the remaining twenty feet into the water below, followed by crumbling rocks. He was still conscious. He swam toward the beach bleeding from his face, like a wounded animal. In an instant, Vladimir disappeared under water; he surged back to the surface gasping for air, screaming. One of the monsters bit down on Vladimir and ripped ferociously side to side. Vladimir's arm and part of his shoulder disappeared. He floated, the crystal-clear water turned, screaming with a last gasp, he shouted, "Lawman you have taken everything from me."

"Only God can take everything from you – I only helped," Jacob shouted.

"A Violent ending to a violent life," Jacob mumbled.

Vladimir's life ended in the stomach of killers. Where it belonged.

Jacob pushed through to the light above, took one last look to see the pieces of the godless murderer floating in a frenzy of sharks, a blood tide from the free-for-all rose onto the sand. Seconds later, the chaos was over, only small pieces of flesh remained.

Jacob crested the opening and pushed through. He stood on the top of the hill overlooking the beach, his beach, his families and his friend's favorite beach. A calm warm feeling covered Jacob's soul. He felt like a warm hand was on his shoulder. Jacob heard a voice, not one verbalized, more in his mind, it wasn't out loud, it was an inner voice but clear as day that said, "I will never leave you nor forsake you."

Chills like never before encompassed Jacob's mind, body and soul. What a great feeling to have, knowing that fact, after all he had been through.

Jacob caught sight of the boat Vladimir sought to run him over with. The boat ran aground on a sand bar fifty feet from shore.

That is fitting, my boat waiting for me, Vladimir gets death. It was the least Vladimir should gift me for all he had done.

Jacob swam out to it without fear, he boarded at the stern, peeked above the transom, no one was aboard, he headed for the wheelhouse. The engine started right up, and he backed it off the sand bar and went west to see if he could find his friends. The boat bounced through the rough water; Below deck a noise caught his attention.

"What next?"

Jacob stopped the boat and searched for a weapon, His father's pocket knife was still in the top drawer and his baseball bat used for clubbing fish was still there. He took them and headed below. To his shock and complete amazement, there was Kate and Xian lying on the floor tied up

Jacob fell back, his eyes bulging out of his head. "Thank God, you both made it,"

"Where did you come from! we thought you were dead," Kate said.

Jacob untied them and bandaged their wounds. "No not dead, it just took me awhile to finish off Vladimir. I finally got him in the caves."

"Thank God it's done; I can't believe Han is not here with us," Xian said. A single tear ran down his face.

"There were none like her; let's go see if we can find her body and give her a proper burial," Jacob said.

"If we can't find her, she would be at ease with a burial at sea – she loved the sea as much as anything," Xian said.

Tears streamed down his face.

Jacob pushed the throttle forward and headed west toward the location of the battle, hoping to find the bodies of Han and Pavel. The area was easy to find; a debris field littered the pacific. The bow of a boat protruding above the water line caught Jacob's attention. The closer Jacob got to the bow of the half-sunk boat he realized it was the *Sea Storm*. Jacob, Kate and Xian scanned the water looking for survivors or bodies and noticed the old life boat a couple hundred yards away.

They didn't see any body from where they were, Jacob pulled the cruiser next to the life boat. All three let out a loud scream. To their shock, laying down on their backs was Pavel and Han bloodied. Xian didn't hesitate he jumped into the lifeboat.

"She is alive, she is alive! Xian said.

"Pavel can you hear me?" Jacob said.

"I hear you," Pavel mumbled.

"What happened?" Jacob said.

"Before the collision I dove out, I found her nearby floating on her back bleeding, but alive, I seen the life boat not far off and dragged her here and bandaged her up, the bullet took off part of her ear and grazed her head. She has a bad headache and is groggy, but she will survive," Pavel said.

"Get them aboard Xian, we need to get to the hospital ASAP," Jacob said.

Jacob spun the cruiser toward port then turned to Kate.

"Kate how are you, you ok?"

"I'm fine. I think we have witnessed a miracle; I assumed Han was dead," Kate said.

"Yeah, me too, I'll feel better once we get everybody safe and at the hospital, then we will deal with your corrupt congressmen. They will pay for what they did to you."

"I want to help," Kate said.

"You will. We won't stop until they're in prison."